THE CHRISTMAS PRESENCE

THE MYSTERY HOUSE SERIES, BOOK FOURTEEN

Eva Pohler

Eva Pohler Books
20011 Park Ranch
San Antonio, Texas 78259
www.evapohler.com

Publisher's Note: This is a work of fiction. Names, characters, places, and incidents are a product of the author's imagination. Locales and public names are sometimes used for atmospheric purposes. Any resemblance to actual people, living or dead, or to businesses, companies, events, institutions, or locales is completely coincidental.

Copy Editor: Alexis Rigoni

Book Cover Design by B Rose DesignZ

THE CHRISTMAS PRESENCE/ Eva Pohler. -- 1st ed.
ISBN: 978-1-958390-82-5

Contents

For the Telluride miners and their families affected by the labor war from 1901-1908.

CHAPTER ONE

The San Juans

Light snowflakes drifted down from the gray sky and gently settled on the windshield as Ellen and her friends made their way up the mountain road. Ellen sat in the back seat of a black Lincoln Navigator, her little black dog, Moseby, nestled comfortably in her lap. She already missed her Santa Fe retreat, where the charm of the adobe buildings and the vibrant art scene had made for a delightful few days with her friends.

"I think I left Mo's food bowl in Santa Fe," she said suddenly from the back seat.

"You want me to turn back?" Sue asked from behind the wheel. "Or will Moseby survive?"

"He'll survive." Ellen scratched her pooch behind the ears. "Won't you, Moseby-Mo?"

Mo pushed his head against her hand for more scratching.

"Your place in Santa Fe is so beautiful, Ellen," Tanya praised from the front passenger's seat as she fiddled with her long, blonde ponytail. "I always forget how much I love it until we're there again."

"It's amazing how much more appeal it has without Suicide Bridge," Sue teased.

Sue referred to a case they had solved a few years ago involving a murderous ghost and restless spirits behind Ellen's Santa Fe retreat.

Ellen pushed her ash blonde hair behind her ears. "I'm glad we were able to work a visit into the trip."

"I felt safer flying into Santa Fe than into Montrose at this time of year," Tanya added. "You never know how bad the snow's going to be up here in Colorado—though driving on these icy roads doesn't seem a whole lot safer."

"Just don't look down, and you'll be fine," Sue promised with a hint of mischief.

As they drove farther, the road steepened, and the scenery became more dramatic. Towering pines dusted with snow lined the path, giving way to breathtaking views of the surrounding mountains. They were nearing their destination, about a mile east of Telluride, and anticipation filled the car.

"I think that's it, just up ahead," Sue said in disbelief, her dark brows disappearing beneath her dark-brown bangs.

"It can't be." Tanya covered her mouth.

"I didn't expect Robin's 'log cabin' to be quite this grand," Sue added, squinting through the falling snow. "This looks more like a mansion."

"Definitely more mansion than cabin," Tanya agreed with a chuckle. "I mean, look at the size of that place!"

Ellen gawked, equally surprised by the size of the structure coming into view. The large, log-constructed home seemed to rise from the mountainside with more glass than logs, a testament to both rustic charm and modern architecture.

As they pulled into the circular driveway—the only part of the landscape not packed with snow—they were greeted by Robin, a woman in her forties with an air of warmth and hospitality, joined by her husband and two kids. The children's eyes were wide with excitement at the sight of Moseby.

"Welcome! We're so glad you could make it," Robin said, her smile bright as she approached the car. "This is my husband, Ken, and our children, Dex and Sophie."

"Nice to meet you," Sue said with a friendly wave.

"Thank you for having us." Ellen stepped out of the car, Moseby jumping down to greet the kids.

With introductions made, the family helped them with their luggage, carrying it just inside the front door, where their own luggage was piled. The children were particularly excited about Moseby, who was more than happy to receive their enthusiastic attention.

"Feel free to pull your car into the garage once we leave," Ken said, following them inside. "And please don't worry about shoveling the driveway. I'll do it again when we come back."

Ellen knew exactly what Sue was thinking as they exchanged glances. Ken's last statement about shoveling was entirely unnecessary. Ellen and her friends had done enough shoveling to last a lifetime—though it usually involved either lost treasure or a body.

"This place is incredible," Tanya said, looking around the spacious interior as they entered. "I love your Christmas tree. It's beautiful."

The tree stood at least ten feet high in the open floor plan next to the dining room and the floor-to-ceiling windows. Decorated in blue and white with white crocheted snowflakes, blue glass ornaments, and cheerful lights, the tree was a breathtaking centerpiece for the room.

"Let me give you a tour," Robin offered. "You'll see why we fell in love with it—all six thousand square feet."

As they walked through the residence, Robin pointed out the features of the five-bedroom, six-bathroom modern home, with its hardwood floors, high cedar ceilings, and sleek, chrome pendant lights. Large windows offered stunning views of Telluride's iconic box canyon and its soaring peaks and cascading waterfalls.

"The house was formed with three horizontal glass pavilions stepped into the mountainside," Robin explained. "The living areas are on this floor, and the bedrooms are upstairs—all but the master. It's downstairs with the game room."

"It's a split-level?" Ellen asked.

"Yes, with the windows downstairs providing a different vantage point," Ken explained. "You really do get a 360-degree view of the surrounding area."

"It's like living in a postcard," Sue said, her voice full of awe.

"Or a snow globe," Ellen chimed in.

Robin smiled. "That's exactly how we feel. The home is adjacent to open space and National Forest land, so we have unobstructed views all around us. Look east and you'll see Ingram and Bridal Veil Falls, the longest free-flowing waterfall in Colorado. And, to the south, you can watch the snow sluff off the steep faces of Ballard Mountain."

"Not to mention the towering aspens and firs," Tanya pointed out.

"I can't believe how beautiful it is," Ellen said, taking in the panoramic views. "No wonder you want to keep it."

The main floor had no interior walls, and two of the adjacent exterior walls were made of floor-to-ceiling windows. The other two adjacent exterior walls, cut into the mountainside, had no windows. The sleek kitchen with its oak cabinets, stainless steel appliances, and black granite island occupied one wall, and a fireplace and television adorned the other. A long dining table for eight was situated between two living areas—one grouped around the fireplace and another across from the kitchen—with its rectangular chandelier creating a visual separation of the spaces. Ellen followed Robin and her friends to the left of the kitchen, where there was a stairwell at the intersection of the two exterior walls that were cut into the mountainside.

"My uncle lived here his whole life, and my grandparents before him—well, not in this particular structure," Robin explained as she led the way. "They lived in a much smaller log cabin on this very spot, and my uncle, too, until five years ago, when he razed the cabin and erected this in its place."

"He did an incredible job," Tanya observed, looking around in admiration as they reached the game room, complete with a pool table, gym, lounge area, and mounted television. Just outside on an expansive terrace was a hot tub, firepit, and outdoor furniture.

"The primary bedroom is through here." Ken gestured for them to enter before him.

Unlike the main floor, the basement was divided in half by an interior wall with the game room on one side and the primary suite on the other. The bathtub was perched right next to a wall of windows with glorious views of cascading falls in the distance.

"What a dream," Ellen said, wondering if she and Brian should think about moving to Colorado.

They followed Robin up the stairs to the top floor, where she showed them an office and four other bedrooms, all with amazing views, even from the bathtubs.

"Feel free to sleep wherever you want," Ken said. "Our *casa* is *su casa*."

"*Gracias*," Tanya said.

As they made their way back to the main floor, Robin said, "When my uncle died six months ago, he left this all to me, having no children of his own. He also left me a note that I'd like you to read."

Once they were back in the main living area, where the children were playing with Moseby on the sofa, Robin handed a piece of paper to Sue, who read it aloud:

"Dearest Robin, I leave you my legacy and hope you and your family will enjoy it as I have. However, you must recall from your childhood that another presence lives here, too. You might remember nightmares, loud noises, and objects falling. I believed leveling the place and starting over might rid me of the curse, but it remained even after the new construction. If you can't share this gorgeous piece of heaven with the darker element, then feel free to sell it. It's yours to do as you wish. Your Loving Uncle, Harold Johnston."

The room fell silent as they absorbed the note's contents.

Ellen finally asked, "How long have you lived here, and what have you experienced?"

Robin and Ken exchanged glances.

"We moved in four months ago," Ken began. "The nightmares started immediately. The dreams are always the same. We're awakened in the dark of night, dragged out of bed, and forced at gunpoint out of the house and up the road in the ice and snow."

"The kids have them, too," Robin added, her voice shaking slightly.

Sue smiled down at the children. "They sound pretty scary."

Sophie nodded. "They *are* scary, even when you wake up in your own bed."

Dex added, "They seem real, too."

"But you can see why we don't want to leave," Ken said. "I've never seen a more beautiful place."

"Likewise," Sue agreed. "And I've seen a lot of beautiful places."

"We'll do everything we can to get to the bottom of this," Ellen promised the family.

"Do you know any other important details about the area's history, particularly if anyone died in the house?" Tanya asked.

Robin nodded. "The old Smuggler-Union Mine Office and Manager's House once sat where this house now stands. One of the managers, Arthur Collins, was shot dead here in the early 1900s."

"That sounds like a good place to start the investigation," Tanya said.

"This house sits on the original cellar," Robin added. "We found a big, plastic tub of my uncle's down there full of papers that might be useful, but between getting moved in, enrolling the kids in a new school, and dealing with these nightmares, we haven't had a chance to go through its contents."

Ellen lifted her brows. "That sounds like another good place to start."

"We'll be staying in a hotel in Telluride." Ken picked up a few suitcases and headed toward the door.

"Call if you have any more questions," Robin added. "And thanks again for doing this. It means so much to me—to all of us."

The children said goodbye to Moseby, and then the young family left the three friends to settle in.

"Is it just me," Sue began, "or is Ken the most beautiful man we've ever seen? I almost introduced myself as Barbie."

Ellen laughed. "Since I have more pairs of readers these days than shoes, I wasn't sure if I could trust my eyes. But, yeah, he's certainly good looking."

Tanya nodded. "I wanted to ask if he could stay and protect us while the rest of his family went to the hotel."

"Now that's the best idea you've had in a long while," Sue chortled.

Suddenly, the row of luggage near the door toppled over with a loud crash.

"This ghost isn't wasting any time," Sue said wryly.

Ellen felt a mix of excitement and apprehension. "Looks like we have our work cut out for us."

"But first we need to see some of the sights," Tanya insisted.

"I think I've already seen the most beautiful sight here," Sue began, her eyes gleaming, "and his name is Ken!"

Ellen held Moseby in her lap as they drove through the picturesque streets of Telluride. The town was dressed for the holidays, with twinkling lights and festive decorations lining the quaint main street. Light snowflakes fell from the sky, adding a touch of magic to the already enchanting scene. Moseby seemed to sense the festive atmosphere, his little tail wagging excitedly as he peered out the window.

"This place is so dog-friendly," Ellen remarked, scratching Moseby's back. "Look at all those people with their dogs. Moseby loves it here, don't you, boy?"

"It's adorable," Sue agreed from the driver's seat. "And look at those lights! It's like something out of a storybook."

Tanya glanced back at Ellen. "I'm surprised to see so many people out on a Monday evening."

They found a parking spot and made their way to Ghost Town Coffee, a cozy little café that promised warmth and delicious treats. The smell of freshly brewed coffee and baked goods greeted them as they stepped inside, Moseby trotting happily at Ellen's side on the end of his leash.

"One cappuccino and a red velvet cupcake, please," Ellen ordered, while Sue and Tanya made their selections. "Oh, and can I have a cup of whipped cream for my pooch?"

Once they had their coffees and an assortment of cupcakes, they settled at a corner table. While Moseby licked happily at his whipped cream, Ellen pulled out her phone and began searching for information about Arthur Collins and the Smuggler-Union Mine.

"Here's something interesting," she said, reading aloud. "Although believed to have been shot by a disgruntled union mine worker, the murder of Arthur Collins was never solved."

Sue leaned in closer. "Do you think that could be the key to our ghost problem?"

"Possibly," Ellen replied before taking a sip of her cappuccino.

Tanya swallowed down the last of her cupcake. "We should definitely look into it further."

After finishing their treats, they made their way to the Telluride Gondola Station. The gondola ride offered stunning views of the snow-covered landscape, and Moseby seemed to enjoy the gentle sway of the cabin as they ascended.

"This is amazing," Sue said, snapping photos of the box canyon below. "Telluride looks so pretty the way it's nestled into the canyon."

"Definitely a highlight of the trip," Tanya agreed. "Though I doubt our husbands would appreciate it as much."

Ellen laughed. "Brian would be more interested in the ski slopes, that's for sure."

They arrived at Mountain Village, a charming resort town that felt like a European village in that it was pedestrian-focused with narrow, cobbled, meandering paths that moved with the landscape. The buildings, crowded together, were a mix of Tudor cottages, chateaus, and stone buildings. Ellen and her friends wandered through shops and galleries, marveling at the variety of art and crafts on display. Ellen bought stuffed animals for her grandbabies—a moose for Brianna, a bighorn mountain sheep for Mason, and an elk for Travis. She also found a pair of earrings she thought her daughter, Alison, would like.

Stopping at the Tomboy Tavern for a beer and burgers, they discussed their next steps.

"I think the Telluride Historical Museum would be a great place to conduct more research," Sue suggested.

"Agreed," Ellen said. "We might find more details about Arthur Collins and why he was shot."

After finishing their dinner, they took the gondola to Market Plaza to buy groceries before getting back on to Telluride, to visit the Telluride Historical Museum.

When they stepped inside, they read a placard that explained that they were standing in the restored 1896 miners' hospital, built by the Western Federation of Miners.

As they browsed the exhibits, Ellen felt a strange sensation, as though someone were standing behind her. She turned quickly, but there was no one there. Shaking off the unsettling feeling, she continued exploring the museum.

"Isn't this cozy?" Tanya remarked on a replica of a miner's cabin. "A single room for sleeping, cooking, dining, and washing up."

"Sounds like they knew how to live it up in luxury," Ellen said before leading them to the next room.

"Dave and I would have divorced years ago if we didn't have separate rooms," Tanya added under her breath.

"You don't mean that." Ellen waved her hand dismissively as they entered the next room.

"I didn't know you had your portrait here," Sue teased Ellen, pointing to a painting of a naked concubine that once worked in the gambling dens of historic Telluride.

"You caught me," Ellen said with a chuckle. "That was one of my previous lives."

"Mine, too," Sue joked. "Except that I had to pay the men instead of the other way around."

"And you would have paid handsomely for Ken," Tanya teased.

"Don't you know it," Sue agreed with a flutter of her lashes.

When Ellen reached Tanya's side, her friend was pointing to a sign that said, "A Medical Curiosity."

"Listen to this," Tanya began, "In 1946, Dr. George G. Balderson made history by being the first doctor to remove his own appendix."

"The first?" Sue repeated. "Does that mean there have been others?"

"That can't have been easy." Ellen shuddered, unable to imagine going through such a thing.

Another exhibit showed an x-ray of a miner's lungs. It was propped up next to a placard discussing miner's consumption. It reminded Ellen of what they'd learned during their case at the Hoover Dam.

Once again, she felt like someone was immediately behind her, but when she turned, she found nothing but air. Tanya stood across the room reading about the early days of the miners' hospital.

"Even though it was the union that raised the money to build the hospital," Tanya started, "from what I'm reading, it sounds like the town had a love-hate relationship with the labor union."

"Can you believe this?" Ellen pointed to a placard that discussed the decline in mining in Telluride and violent strikes in the early 1900s. Ellen read aloud, "Printed in the *Denver Times* on March 7, 1902, Adjutant General Gardner said that the recent avalanches battering Alta, Silver Mountain, Marshall Basin, and Bear Creek were God's vengeance on the organized labor union."

"Tell us what you really think, General," Sue said with a click of her tongue.

As they made their way downstairs and outside to the exhibit of mining cars and large equipment, Ellen whispered to her friends, "I kept feeling like someone was standing behind me, but when I turned, no one was there."

"Same here," Tanya said. "It was really eerie."

"Me too," Sue added. "Looks like our ghost followed us here."

"Unless it's different from the one haunting Robin's house," Tanya noted.

Ellen nodded. "Let's get back and start our investigation."

CHAPTER TWO

First Night

Ellen glanced out the window of Robin's magnificent house, marveling at the snow-covered peaks of the San Juan Mountains shimmering under the brightness of a full moon. She, Sue, and Tanya were still buzzing with excitement from their shopping and sightseeing, and Moseby, exhausted, was curled on the sofa across from a cozy fire that Ellen had built with logs neatly stacked in a stone shelf that receded into the wall near the hearth.

"Well, ladies, time to draw lots for the master bedroom," Sue announced, holding up three straws of varying lengths.

Ellen smirked. "Always the organizer, aren't you, Sue?"

Tanya chuckled. "She still thinks she's our queen."

Sue rolled her eyes but smiled. "Just trying to keep things fair. Now, let's see who gets the royal suite."

Ellen reached out and grabbed a straw, holding it up. It was short. Tanya went next, and her straw was slightly longer. That left Sue with the longest straw, winning her the coveted master bedroom.

"Ha! Looks like the queen gets her castle," Ellen teased.

Sue grinned triumphantly. "It seems some things never change."

Tanya laughed, clapping Sue on the back. "Enjoy your luxury, Your Majesty. We'll make do with the peasants' quarters."

"Like any of us will be missing out," Sue added with a laugh. "There are no losers in this house."

"True," Tanya conceded.

With the sleeping arrangements settled, the trio set about unpacking and setting up their equipment for the night's investigation. Ellen found herself frequently gazing through the windows at the breathtaking views of the surrounding mountains and studying the gorgeous ornaments on the enormous Christmas tree.

As they moved through the main floor, Ellen couldn't shake the feeling that she was being watched. She paused near the kitchen, feeling an inexplicable cold spot that seemed to pierce through her sweater.

"Do you guys feel that?" she asked, rubbing her arms.

Tanya nodded, her brow furrowing. "Yeah, there's definitely something here. It's . . . unsettling."

Sue joined them, holding a digital thermometer. "The temperature just dropped ten degrees in this spot. I think we're onto something."

Ellen glanced around, the hairs on the back of her neck standing on end. "Let's set up the cameras and EMF meters here. This seems to be the hotspot."

They worked quickly, placing their equipment around the main floor, focusing on the areas where the cold spots were most prominent. Sue poured a circle of salt on the hardwood floor around the dining room table and sprinkled it in all the corners. Ellen sprayed holy water like it was air freshener in all three levels of the home before returning to the main floor. Once everything was in place, they gathered around the dining room table, lighting three candles to guide the spirits toward them.

"Alright, let's see if we can make contact," Sue said, her voice steady and calm. "Spirits of the other realm, we come in peace. We mean no harm. We're here to help. I'm Sue."

"I'm Ellen."

"And I'm Tanya."

"If there's anyone here with us," Sue continued, "please give us a sign."

For a moment, there was only silence, and then, from the kitchen, there was a soft thud. They turned to see a book on a low shelf built into the kitchen island topple over. Ellen's heart raced, a mix of fear and excitement coursing through her veins as she gripped the *gris gris* bag around her neck.

Moseby, still curled on the nearby couch, whined.

"Did you see that?" Ellen whispered to her friends.

Sue nodded and addressed the spirits, "Did you push over that book? If so, please knock once for yes and twice for no."

They waited, holding their breath. After a pause they heard a knock.

"Yes!" Tanya whispered.

At that moment, one of their cat ball devices on the kitchen island began illuminating with brightly colored lights—something that only happened when the device was touched.

The friends exchanged looks of excitement.

Sue cleared her throat. "Are you the ghost of Arthur Collins, the Smuggler-Union mine manager who was shot here in 1902? Please knock once for yes and twice for no."

After a pause, there were two distinct knocks. Ellen exchanged a puzzled look with Tanya and Sue.

"Okay, not Arthur Collins," Sue said. "Let's see if we can get a name. Ellen, grab the Ouija board."

Ellen retrieved the board from her bag and placed it on the table. The three of them positioned their fingertips lightly on the planchette. After "opening" the board, Sue cleared her throat.

"Is there anyone here who would like to communicate with us?" Sue asked.

The planchette began to move slowly, spelling out S-A-I-N-T.

"Saint?" Tanya frowned. "Are we talking to a saint?"

The planchette moved to "NO," leaving them even more confused.

"What could 'saint' mean then?" Ellen wondered aloud. "Is 'Saint' your name?"

The planchette moved to "YES."

"What's your last name, Saint?" Sue asked.

When the planchette failed to move again, Ellen felt discouraged.

"We need more information," Sue said. "Let's close the board and try the Estes Method. Tanya, are you ready?"

Tanya nodded, putting on a blindfold and slipping the headphones over her ears. The headphones were connected to her spirit box app, which shuffled radio broadcasts, believed to be manipulated by spirits.

"Who are you?" Ellen asked, her voice steady despite the growing tension in the room.

"Hello," Tanya said.

"Hello," Ellen replied. "Can you tell us your name? I'm Ellen."

"Saint," Tanya said.

"Your name is Saint?" Sue asked.

Tanya remained silent.

Ellen repeated her question.

Tanya said, "John."

"Your name is John?" Sue asked.

Tanya gave no reply.

"Why haven't you moved on?" Ellen asked.

"Protect," Tanya said. "Family."

"You're here to protect the family?" Ellen asked.

"That doesn't make sense," Sue whispered. "The family is being terrorized."

"Unless there is more than one spirit here," Ellen pointed out.

Tanya's face remained expressionless beneath the blindfold as she said, "Barney. Collins. Buck. Blame."

Ellen and Sue exchanged baffled glances.

"Arthur Collins?" Ellen whispered.

"Innocent," Tanya continued.

Beneath her breath, Sue said, "This spirit has a lot to say."

Ellen leaned forward, feeling the weight of the words. "Is there more than one spirit present?"

"Yes," Tanya said immediately. "Help me."

"Can you tell us who we're speaking to?" Ellen asked.

"Buck," Tanya said. Then she added, "Wells."

Sue took up her phone and looked up Buck Wells.

Then, more forcefully, Tanya said, "He's guilty!"

Tanya suddenly pulled off the blindfold and headphones, her eyes wide with fear. "The voice sounded so angry."

Ellen put a comforting hand on Tanya's shoulder, since she was trembling with fear. "It's okay. You did great."

Sue nodded in agreement. "We got a name—Buck Wells. He was the Smuggler-Union mine manager who replaced Arthur Collins after Arthur was shot."

Ellen and Tanya exchanged looks of surprise.

"Could Wells have shot Collins?" Ellen wondered aloud. "Sounds like he had a motive."

Just then, all three candles went out, causing the three friends to jump back in their chairs. Moseby came over to Ellen and whined at her feet.

"It's okay, Moseby-Mo," she cooed as she lifted him into her lap.

"Why don't we call it a night," Sue suggested. "We have a big day ahead of us tomorrow, and I need my beauty sleep."

"Yes, my queen," Tanya teased.

The friends turned off their equipment, along with the main floor lights. Robin had said to leave the Christmas tree lights on, and they were even lovelier in the dark. Ellen took Moseby outside to pee once more before returning inside and locking the door. As she made her way upstairs with Moseby, Ellen couldn't shake the feeling that they were being watched. She glanced back one last time before heading into her room, the shadows of the house seeming to move just beyond her line of sight.

As Ellen lay in what she believed was Sophie's bed with her face washed, her teeth brushed, and her clothes changed, she replayed the events of the evening in her mind. The cold spots, the knocks, the strange words from the Estes Method—they all pointed to something unsettled in the house. After a brief phone call with Brian, she plugged in her phone to its charger and settled under the covers. She hoped that tomorrow would bring more answers, but, for now, she tried to find comfort in the familiar feeling of Moseby curled beside her on the bed.

Sleep came slowly, her mind a whirl of possibilities and unanswered questions. But one thing was certain: they were not alone in this house, and whatever was here had a story to tell. Ellen was determined to uncover it, no matter what it took.

A harsh light shone on Ellen's face, piercing the darkness and her dreams. A gruff voice shattered the silence. "Get up! Get out of bed!"

Terrified, Ellen bolted upright, her heart pounding in her chest. She grabbed Moseby, clutching him to her as she tried to make sense of the situation. Standing in her room were three armed men, their faces shadowed by the glare of their flashlights. As she climbed from her bed, her knees almost buckled beneath her.

"What do you want? Take anything, but please don't hurt me and my friends," she pleaded, her voice wavering.

"Stop talking and start walking," one of the men barked, pointing his gun at her.

Ellen, shaking from head to toe, obeyed, clutching Moseby more closely. She made her way downstairs, where she saw Sue and Tanya held at gunpoint by two other men. The sight of her friends in such peril filled her with a desperate fear.

All three women were forced outside into the icy cold, their bare feet sinking into the snow. The biting chill of the snow and ice beneath Ellen's feet felt like walking on sharp needles, but there was no relief to be found. Snow was everywhere, relentless and unforgiving.

"Where are you taking us?" Ellen asked, her voice barely more than a whisper.

"Just keep walking," one of the armed men insisted.

They were made to march up a steep incline along the side of the mountain. The drop below was so abrupt that Ellen feared she could slip and fall into the abyss. Holding Moseby more tightly against her, she clung to the side of the mountain, her friends sobbing behind her.

As afraid as she was for her own well-being, Ellen's heart ached for Sue, who found it difficult to hike with her bad knees and feet. How would she make the treacherous hike without falling to her death? Ellen's own knee was stiff, causing her to limp.

"Please?" Ellen begged the men behind them. "What is the meaning of this?"

"Shut your trap and keep walking," one of the men growled.

The trail opened up to an icy wooden bridge, perilously suspended over a deep chasm.

"Go on," the man ordered. "Leave and don't come back."

Another of the armed men added, "If we see you around here again, we'll shoot first and ask questions later."

Ellen and her friends gingerly crossed the icy bridge. Her feet had become so numb that Ellen could no longer feel them. Suddenly, a gunshot rang out, and Ellen and her friends jumped in fright. Sue slipped on the ice and tumbled over the side.

"Sue!" Ellen cried, hysterically sobbing now. "No!"

She and Tanya clung to one another as tears streamed down their faces.

"Why'd you shoot, you dumb-ass?" one of the men grumbled.

"The big elephant is about to slide!" another of the men shouted. "Let's get out of here!"

Suddenly, the mountain quaked, and a roar like a train echoed through the peaks. Ellen noticed a mound of white snow sliding down the mountain directly headed for her and Tanya. With a gasp, she woke up just as the snow was enveloping her, finding herself in bed with Moseby, safe in Robin's house. She was gasping for air and shaking uncontrollably.

Realizing it had been a nightmare, she wondered how on earth Robin and her family had endured such terrifying dreams for four months. It had seemed so real.

"I'll be right back," she whispered to Moseby before heading downstairs for a drink of water. After filling a glass at the kitchen sink and taking several gulps, she felt the hair on the back of her neck rise as a chill swept up her spine.

She turned to see two shadowy figures locked in hand-to-hand combat before the hearth, their outlines barely visible in front of the dying embers now nothing more than an orange glow. Ellen covered her mouth, unable to breathe, as she watched in silence. Then, the figures fell to the floor and disappeared.

CHAPTER THREE

Falls

Ellen woke Tuesday morning to the aroma of fresh coffee and the soft murmur of voices in the kitchen. She blinked sleepily at the sunlight streaming through the window. The views of snow-covered firs, aspens, pines, and cypresses, along with a cascading waterfall in the distance, took her breath away. What an amazing sight to wake up to. Moseby was curled up beside her, still dozing. She gave him a gentle pat before slipping out of bed.

Wrapping her robe around herself, Ellen padded downstairs with Moseby on her heels. She found Sue and Tanya already seated at the kitchen bar, steaming mugs of coffee in hand and a box of doughnuts between them.

"Morning, Ellen," Sue greeted with a warm smile. "Sleep well?"

Ellen hesitated, a shiver running down her spine as she recalled her harrowing nightmare. "Morning. It was . . . eventful, to say the least."

"Eventful?" Tanya raised an eyebrow. "That sounds intriguing."

"Hold that thought," Ellen said. "Let me take Moseby out first. He probably needs to pee."

Grabbing Moseby's leash, Ellen headed outside. The crisp morning air nipped at her cheeks, and the snow crunched beneath her slippers, reminding her of the treacherous climb in her nightmare. Moseby sniffed around, finally finding a spot to do his business. Ellen soaked in the serene beauty surrounding Robin's property, trying to calm her racing thoughts.

Once Moseby was done, she led him back inside, where the warmth of the kitchen was a welcome relief. She joined her friends at the table, pouring herself a cup of coffee and selecting a doughnut.

"So, about my night," Ellen began, taking a sip of coffee. "I had this horrible nightmare. There were these armed men who forced us out of the house and made us walk up the mountain in our bare feet. It felt so real."

Sue and Tanya exchanged glances, their expressions mirroring Ellen's unease.

"That's strange," Tanya said slowly. "I had a similar dream. We were being marched over an icy bridge by armed bandits. I woke up feeling like I was still at gunpoint."

Sue nodded. "Me too. Except in mine, we were trapped in a cave as an avalanche fell over the mouth, blocking us in. I was disappointed that Ken wasn't there in the dream with me. He would have made it less of a nightmare, for sure."

Despite Sue's attempt at humor, Ellen felt a chill that had nothing to do with the temperature. "I wonder if the spirits are trying to tell us something with these dreams, or if we're just experiencing the same nightmare they've been trapped in since their deaths."

"I don't know," Sue said thoughtfully.

"I did a little research on my phone last night," Tanya revealed. "I think the dreams are related to the forceful removal of union mine workers by the Citizen's Alliance in 1904. It seems the people of Telluride were tired of the union's antics and wanted the troublemakers driven out of town."

"That's good work, Tanya," Ellen praised.

"But why are we experiencing the nightmares from the perspective of the troublemakers?" Sue wondered aloud.

"We need to do more research," Tanya pointed out.

Ellen nodded, taking a bite of her doughnut. "We need to find out more about Buck Wells. He's the best lead we have so far."

Sue pulled out her laptop and opened a new tab. "We're still visiting Ouray today, right? Apparently, they have a nice library. Maybe after our sightseeing, we could talk to one of the librarians for help."

"I'll call ahead and see if we can set up an appointment," Tanya said, reaching for her phone.

"Good thinking, Tanya." Ellen felt excited about their prospects.

"Speaking of a presence taking over the house," Sue began. "Did I tell you that Luke has moved back home so he can focus on getting his master's degree?"

"No," Tanya said before pulling out her phone. "No more empty nest for you, then."

"Not only that," Sue continued, "his fiancée's visa, which was supposed to take a year to get, should be ready next month."

"So?" Ellen asked. "Does that mean she'll be moving in, too?"

Sue slapped her hands on the bar. "Well, we thought she'd be coming from Mexico next year, when he'd have his degree and could get a job and support them, but that's not what's happening. She'll be moving in right after Christmas and get this: He wants us to let them have the master bedroom!"

"He's had you and Tom wrapped around his little finger his whole life," Tanya said with a laugh. "I bet he gets what he wants. What do you think, Ellen?"

"I think Luke's ability to take over Sue's house is more powerful than any ghost's!"

Ellen and her group arrived in the adorable town of Ouray shortly after nine o'clock, their spirits high despite the lingering unease from their previous night's dreams. The quaint town, nestled in the San Juan Mountains, offered a charming escape with its historic buildings and stunning natural beauty. Ellen could see why it was called "The Switzerland of America."

Their first stop was a hike to see the Box Canyon Springs. However, as they approached the trailhead, a sign made it clear that dogs weren't allowed. Ellen frowned, glancing down at Moseby, who wagged his tail innocently.

"I guess I'll have to stay behind with Moseby," Sue said with exaggerated reluctance, already eyeing a nearby bench.

Ellen and Tanya exchanged amused glances. Sue's dislike of strenuous activities was well known, and this was the perfect excuse for her to avoid the hike.

"Sue, you don't have to make such a big sacrifice," Ellen teased, her lips twitching into a smile.

Sue grinned. "Well, someone has to do it. You two go on ahead. Moseby and I will hold down the fort here."

With a chuckle, Ellen and Tanya set off, leaving Sue and Moseby behind. The trail to Box Canyon Springs led them down a series of steel stairs and walkways that snaked their way into the canyon. It was hard for Ellen in some places, but Tanya was patient, waiting for her to catch up. The sound of rushing water grew louder with each step, filling the air with a refreshing mist.

As they descended, the view opened up to reveal the breathtaking Box Canyon Falls. The water cascaded down the rocky cliffs, creating a mesmerizing display of raw, natural power. The sunlight filtered through the trees, casting shimmering rainbows in the spray.

"This is incredible," Tanya said, her eyes wide with wonder.

Ellen's gaze was fixed on the falls. "It's beautiful. I can see why this place is so popular."

They continued along the walkway, marveling at the sheer cliffs that towered above them and the lush greenery that clung to the rocks. The steel stairs took them down into the heart of the canyon, where the falls roared with a deafening intensity, before leading them back up to the top. It was a challenging hike, but the views made every step worth it, and Tanya, ever patient, allowed Ellen to take her time.

When they finally rejoined Sue and Moseby, they found Sue deep in conversation with a man who looked to be in his seventies with a weathered face and a twinkle in his eye.

"You two missed out on a riveting history lesson," Sue said, a hint of mischief in her voice. "This is Hank. He's lived here all his life and knows a thing or two about Buck Wells and the mining days."

Hank tipped his hat. "Pleasure to meet you, ladies. I was just telling your friend here about my great-great-uncle. He was a mine owner back when the Western Federation of Miners, known as the 63, was causing all sorts of trouble. The head of the federation was a man named Vincent St. John. Folks called him Saint for short."

Ellen's eyes widened. "Saint? That's one of our ghosts!"

Tanya clapped her hands. "Good work, Sue! This is exactly what we needed."

Sue beamed with pride. "I guess it was a good thing we hung back, right Moseby?"

Ellen laughed, taking Moseby's leash. "Thanks, Sue. Let's head to the rental car and check out Cascade Falls next." Then she turned to Hank. "Nice to meet you. Have a great day!"

They drove a few miles into town and parked at the trailhead for Cascade Falls. The hike was shorter, but no less rewarding, and still a challenge for Ellen and Sue. The trail wound through dense forest, the air cool and crisp. After about a mile, they reached the falls, which tumbled down a series of rocky steps, creating a remarkable scene. They paused a moment to catch their breath and take photos, and then they found another hiker to get a shot of all three of them, plus the pooch.

With the photos taken, Ellen stood in awe, the sound of the water a soothing backdrop to her thoughts. "It's amazing how much beauty is packed into this little town."

Tanya nodded, snapping more pictures with her phone. "And to think, all this history too."

After spending some time taking in the view and recovering from the hike, they returned to town and walked down Main Street, admiring the holiday décor and quaint storefronts. A few blocks over, they arrived at Mi Mexico, a cozy Mexican food restaurant with excellent reviews.

The warm, spicy aroma of the food greeted them as they stepped inside. They were seated at a corner booth, where they eagerly perused the menu.

"This place smells amazing," Ellen said, her stomach growling.

"According to the reviews," Sue began, "the shrimp enchiladas are to die for."

"Oh, that's exactly what I want," Tanya announced.

Ellen smiled down at Moseby, feeling a sense of contentment. Despite the strange occurrences and unsettling dreams, moments like these—exploring new places and uncovering pieces of history with her friends—made it all worthwhile.

As they enjoyed their meal, they discussed their next steps, fueled by the new lead about Saint. Ellen felt a renewed sense of determination. They were getting closer to understanding the mystery, and hopefully their appointment with the Ouray librarian would shed even more light on the ghosts haunting Robin's magnificent house.

After their dinner, the trio and dog strolled the few blocks from Mi Mexico Restaurant to the Ouray Colorado Public Library. The cool mountain air was invigorating, and the cute streets of Ouray, lined with buildings decorated for the holidays and lightly dusted with snow, added to the charming atmosphere of their afternoon adventure.

"I love that we never argue over where we're going to eat or what we're going to do on these trips," Tanya said, seemingly out of the blue. "With Dave, everything is a fight these days."

"Traveling with men is never as much fun as traveling with women," Ellen agreed.

"Speak for yourself," Sue teased. "It depends on the men. I'd go anywhere with Ken."

As they approached the library, Ellen admired the building's historic architecture. The red-brick structure with its arched windows and welcoming entrance added to the surrounding charm.

Inside, they were greeted by the soft hum of activity typical of a small-town library. Ellen glanced around, taking in the cozy reading nooks and the rows of bookshelves that promised a wealth of information. They made their way to the reference desk, where a tall, lean man with bright blue eyes behind wire-rimmed glasses stood waiting.

"Hello, are you Leon?" Ellen asked.

"Indeed, I am."

Ellen extended her hand. "I'm Ellen, and these are my friends, Tanya and Sue. Tanya spoke to you on the phone earlier today."

Leon shook her hand with a warm smile. "It's a pleasure to meet you."

The women nodded in greeting, and Moseby panted from his cloth pooch carrier, as if introducing himself, too.

Leon chuckled. "And who's this little fellow?"

"This is Moseby," Ellen said with a fond smile. "He's part of the team."

"Well, it's good to have all of you here," Leon said. "I've pulled some books from the stacks that discuss what history has called 'the reign of terror' from 1889 to 1908 caused by the Western Federation of Miners. It's a dark period in our history but fascinating, nonetheless."

Leon led them to a nearby table where several books were stacked neatly. He began to explain, "I don't know much about the topic personally, except for what I've learned in school. The miners faced extremely harsh conditions, and when they went on strike, non-unionized workers, called scabs by the union, were brought in to keep the mines operational. This led to a lot of violence, and many miners lost their lives."

Ellen picked up one of the books, its worn cover indicating years of use. She flipped through the pages, scanning the chapter titles. "This is exactly what we need. Thank you, Leon."

"My pleasure," he said. "I can help you get a library card if you'd like to check these out."

"That would be great," Ellen replied.

They followed the librarian to the front desk, where he handed Ellen a form to fill out. As she completed the necessary information, she couldn't help but feel a sense of anticipation. Each new piece of information brought them one step closer to understanding the mysteries they were unraveling.

Leon processed the form quickly and handed Ellen her new library card. "There you go. You're all set. You can check out the books now."

Ellen smiled as she handed the books to Leon, who scanned them and returned them to her. "Thank you so much for your help, Leon. This really means a lot to us."

"You're welcome," he said. "If you need any more information or have any questions, feel free to call or stop by."

Ellen and her friends expressed their gratitude once more before heading out of the library, books in hand. As they walked back to their car, Ellen felt excited. The pieces of the puzzle were starting to come together, and she was eager to dive into the books and learn more about Buck Wells and the turbulent history of the Western Federation of Miners.

The drive back to Telluride was filled with discussions about what they hoped to find in the books. Ellen was particularly interested in any mentions of Vincent St. John, the man known as "Saint," who had played a pivotal role in the miners' struggles and who was now haunting Robin's house, along with Buck Wells.

Back in Telluride, Ellen and her friends drove to Dante's Mountain Tours for their appointment to see Bridal Veil Falls, Bear Pass, and the Pandora ghost town.

As they approached the tour office, they were greeted by Dante, a rugged, affable man in his forties with a sunburnt face and a broad smile.

"Welcome, folks! Ready for an afternoon of adventure?" he asked.

"Absolutely," Ellen replied, feeling Moseby tugging excitedly at his leash. "We can't wait to see the sights."

They climbed into a large, sturdy Jeep, which rumbled to life with a powerful growl.

Sue settled into her seat with a sigh of relief. "I have to say, hiking in the mountains is much nicer when a large Jeep does most of the work for you," she quipped, causing everyone to laugh.

The Jeep made its way up the winding mountain roads, offering stunning views of the surrounding peaks and valleys. As they climbed higher, the air grew cooler and crisper, the scent of pine filling their lungs.

Their first stop was Bridal Veil Falls, a breathtaking cascade of water tumbling down a sheer cliff. The Jeep parked near the base of the falls, and they all stepped out to take in the view. The roar of the falls was thunderous, and the mist created a shimmering rainbow in the sunlight.

"This is incredible," Tanya said, snapping pictures with her phone. "I can't believe how beautiful it is."

Ellen nodded, feeling a sense of reverence. "It's like something out of a fairy tale."

"Robin said it's the longest free-flowing waterfall in Colorado," Sue reminded them as she, too, took several photos. "Let's get a picture together for our scrapbooks."

Dante offered to take it, so they moved closer with Tanya in the middle, their arms wrapped around one another's waists.

After a while, they piled back into the Jeep and continued their journey. Dante expertly navigated the rugged terrain, sharing anecdotes and bits of history about the area. The next leg of their tour took them through Bear Pass, where the narrow, winding roads offered heart-stopping views of the valleys below.

As they climbed higher, Sue couldn't resist making another joke. "I think I'm finally starting to appreciate nature—mainly because I'm not the one doing the climbing!"

Their laughter echoed through the mountains, a light-hearted counterpoint to the rugged landscape.

Finally, they reached the Pandora ghost town. The Jeep came to a stop near the ruins of old cabins. The air was thick with the history of the place, and Moseby seemed particularly interested in exploring, pulling eagerly at his leash.

"Feel free to have a look around," Dante said. "Take as much time as you need. I'm never in a hurry to leave this place. It's a piece of my personal history. My great-great-grandfather lived in that house just over there." He pointed to a ruin in the distance.

"What's your family name?" Sue asked.

"Zadra. It's Italian," Dante replied. "My family has been here for over a century. My great-great-grandfather came over as a young man in 1883."

Moseby pulled impatiently at his leash.

"Let's go, Moseby," Ellen said, letting him lead the way.

The little dog trotted happily across the grounds, sniffing at the ruins and wagging his tail.

The group wandered around the ghost town, marveling at the eerie remnants of a bygone era. As Ellen followed Moseby around the back of one of the crumbling cabins, she suddenly stopped short. Standing before her was what she first mistook for a man, but soon realized was a full-body apparition. The ghostly figure was dressed in tattered clothes and boots. His eyes were hollow, and his face was a mask of grim determination.

"He deserved what he got," the apparition said, his voice thick with an accent Ellen didn't recognize.

"Who did?" Ellen asked, but the figure vanished, leaving her shaken and breathless. She stood there for a moment, trying to process what she had just seen and heard. Moseby, sensing her distress, whined softly and nudged her leg.

"Let's go back to the others," Ellen whispered, her heart pounding. She made her way back to the group, still reeling from the encounter.

Sue and Tanya noticed her pale face immediately.

"Ellen, are you okay?" Tanya asked, concern etched in her features.

"I . . . I saw something," Ellen stammered, her voice trembling. "A ghost. He said, 'He deserved what he got' and then vanished."

The gravity of her words hung in the air as they climbed back into the Jeep. On the ride back down to the parking lot, Ellen recounted her experience in detail. Dante listened intently, his usual jovial demeanor replaced by a serious expression.

"Well, you're not the first to see something strange up there," he said finally. "The place has a lot of history, and not all of it's pretty."

As they drove down the mountain, the sun began to dip behind the peaks, casting beautiful colors of pink and lavender across the landscape. Ellen looked out at the splendor, her mind racing. The apparition's message was clear: there were secrets buried in these mountains.

Back at the tour office, they thanked Dante and made their way to their rental car. Moseby, exhausted from the day's adventures, curled up in the back seat with Ellen, while she and her friends discussed their next steps.

"Maybe we'll find something useful in these books Leon recommended," Tanya pointed out.

As they drove back to their temporary home, the mountain peaks silhouetted against the twilight sky, Ellen was anxious to continue their research.

CHAPTER FOUR

The Bin

Ellen sighed contentedly as she finished the last bite of her sandwich. It had been a long day of adventure and discovery, and now, freshly showered and changed into comfortable pajamas, she was ready to unwind. Moseby lay curled at the foot of the bed, his eyes half-closed.

Ellen picked up one of the library books recommended by Leon, the Ouray librarian. The book, a detailed account of the Western Federation of Miners and the tumultuous events of the late 19th and early 20th centuries, promised to shed light on the mysteries they were unraveling.

She had just settled into her pillows and started reading when Moseby suddenly perked up. The little dog jumped off the bed, his nails clicking on the hardwood floor as he trotted out of the room. Ellen watched him curiously, wondering what had caught his attention. Moments later, she heard him running down the stairs.

"What is it, Moseby?" she called out, setting the book aside and following him. "Do you need to go outside?"

She followed him down to the basement. Not sure if Sue had gone to bed, Ellen whispered, "Moseby, come on."

Instead of listening to her, he pawed at a door at the back of the game room.

Ellen hesitated for a moment, then twisted the knob. The door creaked open to reveal a set of wooden steps leading down into darkness. She felt a shiver of apprehension. Moseby whined again, looking back at her with wide, anxious eyes.

"Wait here," she told him, turning back to her room to grab her phone. She turned on the flashlight app, and, with the beam cutting through the darkness, she began her descent. Moseby remained at the top of the stairs, whining softly.

The steps were cold beneath her bare feet, and the air grew cooler and mustier as she descended. She shivered in the darkness, wondering if one of the ghosts dwelled there. At the bottom, the flashlight revealed a small, dusty cellar with a dirt floor. The square room was empty, so what had provoked Moseby? She was about to leave when she noticed a door in the back, its wood weathered, and its handle worn. It looked out of place in the opulent building, like something ancient. She pulled on the handle, but the door wouldn't budge. She tried a few more times, tugging with all her might, and finally got it open.

Shining her light into the dark chamber, she found a dusty, plastic bin about two feet long, high, and deep on the dirt floor. Believing it to be the tub Robin had mentioned—and Ellen had forgotten about— she pried it open and discovered papers, letters, and a worn journal.

She carefully lifted the journal, its leather cover cracked and brittle with age. The name on the first page made her heart race: Arthur Lancelot Collins. She couldn't believe her eyes. This journal might hold the key to the mysteries they were investigating.

Ellen hurried back upstairs, her excitement barely contained. She found Tanya and Sue in the kitchen, chatting over cups of hot tea in their pajamas.

"Guys, you have to see this," Ellen said breathlessly. "I found the plastic bin Robin mentioned before she left. I'd forgotten all about it."

"Oh, so did I," Sue exclaimed.

Ellen caught her breath. "Among newspaper clippings, documents, and letters, I found a journal that belonged to Arthur Collins!"

Tanya and Sue exchanged surprised looks, then followed Ellen back to the cellar door. Ellen led the way down the steps, with Tanya and Sue close behind. Moseby stayed at the top, still uneasy about the dark space below.

"Let's bring the tub up," Ellen said. "There's so much here to comb through."

Sue held her phone flashlight on the stairs while Ellen and Tanya carefully lifted the bin together and carried it up to the game room. They placed it beside the coffee table and began to sort through the contents.

"I thought Robin said they were her uncle's letters," Sue said with a touch of excitement. "But these look like they belonged to Arthur Collins or Buck Wells."

"Look at this," Ellen said, holding up a yellowed newspaper clipping. "It's dated August 8, 1907, from the *Telluride Daily Journal*. The headline reads: 'Barney's Bones are Found.'"

Tanya and Sue leaned in to read the subheading: "Skeleton of Bullion Shift Boss is Recovered; Seven Years Search Bears Results; Remains of W.J. Barney, Brutally Murdered by St. John and his Fellows June 22, 1901, are Recovered."

Sue straightened up, her expression grim. "So, St. John was a murderer, and he's haunting this house?"

As if in response, a lamp standing in the corner of the room suddenly toppled over, crashing to the floor. All three women flinched, and Moseby let out a frightened yelp.

"Okay, that's definitely not a coincidence," Tanya said, her voice trembling slightly.

Ellen took a deep breath, trying to steady her nerves. "We need to figure out what happened back then. Why did St. John kill Barney, and why is he haunting us now?"

They continued to sift through the papers, finding more pieces of the puzzle. The letters revealed tensions between the miners and the mine owners, and the journal provided a personal account of the events leading up to the murder.

"This confirms what Hank told us—that St. John was a leader in the miners' union," Ellen said, reading aloud from the journal. "Collins wrote that Saint believed Barney to be a Pinkerton operative for the mine owners, and there were rumors that Barney was sabotaging the union's efforts."

"Pinkerton?" Sue echoed. "Like the detective agency in that Netflix show?"

Ellen shrugged. "I don't know."

"But to kill him?" Tanya asked, shaking her head. "That's extreme."

"Desperate times, desperate measures," Sue said, her eyes scanning another letter. "Still, murder is murder."

Ellen felt a chill run down her spine. She looked at the fallen lamp and then back at her friends. "Whatever happened back then, it's clear these spirits have unfinished business."

They continued to work late into the night, piecing together the tragic story of the miners' conflict. Ellen began to uncover contradictory information from two different newspapers. The *Telluride Daily Journal* reported on Vincent St. John and the union's disruptive behavior in Telluride, accusing him and his men of assault, vandalism, and murder. The journal corroborated the article, describing an unprovoked attack by several hundred armed, masked men on the Smuggler-Union buildings with valuable property destroyed, along with the life of one John Barthell. However, an article printed in the *San Miguel Examiner* on July 13, 1901, claimed that the conflict was not sought by the union men, who maintained a peaceable stand all along. The union officers had no foreknowledge of events leading to gunfire and death and weren't even on the property of the mine the morning the disturbance occurred. It went on to say that St. John risked his own life to stop the riot and that a non-union worker named Bill Jordan, deputized by the Mine Owners' Association, was the one that witnesses say shot John Barthell. More and more articles from the *Telluride Daily Journal* implicated St. John while as many articles from the *San Miguel Examiner* vindicated him. Which paper was reporting the truth?

As they prepared to call it a night, Ellen looked around at the scattered papers that still held untold secrets. "We've got a lot of work ahead of us, but I think we're on the right track."

"We need our sleep for tomorrow's adventures," Tanya pointed out. "I can't keep my eyes open anymore."

Sue climbed to her feet. "We can take some of these documents with us to read on the train."

"Good idea, Sue," Ellen said.

"I hear that a lot," Sue teased. "Good night."

"Good night," Ellen and Tanya replied.

"Don't let the bed bugs bite," Sue added with a lift of her brows.

Ellen was jolted awake by the harsh sound of a man's voice. Blinking against the sudden brightness of the flashlight shining in her face, she tried to make sense of what was happening. An armed man stood at the foot of her bed, his gun trained on her.

"Get up," he ordered, his voice low and menacing. "Out of bed, now."

Heart pounding, Ellen scrambled out of bed, her first thought racing to Moseby. She glanced around frantically, but her dog was nowhere to be seen.

"Where's Moseby?" she asked, her voice quaking with fear.

"Moseby?" the man repeated roughly.

"My dog."

The gunman's expression didn't change. "I don't care about your dog. Move."

Panicked, Ellen fled the room and rushed down the stairs. Moseby was nowhere to be found, and neither were her friends.

"Where are my friends?" she asked the man on her heels.

"Stop talking and start walking," he growled, prodding her with the barrel of his gun.

Barefoot, Ellen stepped out of the front door and onto the cold, icy driveaway. She was led outside into the frigid night, the cold biting into her skin. The snow beneath her feet was freezing cold, causing sharp pain with every step. Just as the overwhelming fear and confusion threatened to consume her, she woke up, gasping for breath.

Heart racing, Ellen looked around, relief washing over her as she saw Moseby curled up beside her. She pulled him close, hugging him tightly. "Just a nightmare," she whispered to herself, trying to calm her racing heart. "It was just a nightmare."

But before she could fully relax, the bedroom door burst open again. Several armed men entered, their guns pointed at her. Ellen's blood turned to ice. This couldn't be happening. Not again.

"Out of bed, now!" one of the men barked.

With Moseby scooped up in her arms, Ellen obeyed, desperately hoping this was still part of her dream. She was led downstairs, her knees week and trembling. On the main floor, she saw Sue and Tanya, similarly treated and equally terrified.

Fear gripped Ellen's heart. This felt too real to be a dream. The three friends were forced out into the freezing night, their bare feet sinking into the snow. They were made to march up a steep, treacherous mountain path. Ellen stumbled, her grip on Moseby slipping.

"Keep moving!" one of the men shouted.

As Ellen struggled to regain her footing, she lost her hold on Moseby. The little dog tumbled over the side of the path, falling into the dark abyss below. Ellen screamed, her heart shattering as she watched him disappear.

"No!" she cried out, the sound of her own voice waking her once again. She was back in bed, drenched in sweat, her heart pounding wildly in her chest. Moseby was curled beside her, safe and sound.

Ellen hugged him tightly, tears streaming down her face. "It was just a dream," she whispered, trying to convince herself.

But the terror wasn't over. An armed man walked into her room, and Ellen's heart skipped a beat. Was this another nightmare? She needed to know. Desperate, she decided to test if it was a dream by attempting to fly.

Concentrating hard, she felt herself lift off the bed, soaring over the armed man who fired his gun at her. Bullets whizzed past, but she and Moseby dodged them easily. Relief washed over her as she confirmed it wasn't really happening.

"It's just a dream," she told herself, dodging another bullet. "Everything is okay."

Ellen kept flying, maneuvering around the room as the man continued to shoot at her. The dream felt vivid and real, but she knew she had control. She focused on her breathing, trying to steady her nerves. The sensation of flying, combined with the adrenaline from the dream, created an eerie mix of fear and exhilaration.

Eventually, the scene began to fade, the man and the room dissolving into darkness. Ellen's eyes fluttered open, and she found herself back in bed, Moseby nestled comfortably beside her. Her heart was still racing, but she was awake, really awake this time. She knew it because she tried to fly and couldn't.

She lay there for a long moment, holding Moseby close, trying to process the layers of nightmares she had just experienced. The fear, the relief, the confusion—it all felt overwhelming.

"It's okay, Moseby," she murmured—more to herself than to him—as she stroked his fur. "We're safe."

She took several deep breaths, letting the reality of the present moment ground her. As the adrenaline slowly left her system, exhaustion took its place. Ellen closed her eyes, determined to get some rest despite the lingering fear.

In the quiet of the night, with Moseby's steady breathing beside her, Ellen finally drifted back to sleep, hoping for a dreamless slumber.

CHAPTER FIVE

The Train to Silverton

Ellen and her friends woke early Wednesday morning to make the most of their journey to Silverton. After coffee and bagels, they packed into their rental car with Moseby in tow and set off for Durango to make the eight o'clock train. Upon arrival, they boarded the Durango-Silverton for a round-trip scenic ride through the majestic San Juan Mountains. The train ride promised a day filled with breathtaking, snowy views and an opportunity to delve deeper into the history they were unraveling.

Settled comfortably in a cabin on the train, Ellen positioned herself next to a window, Moseby nestled warmly in his cloth pooch carrier strapped across her and resting in her lap. The scenery outside was nothing short of magical: snow-covered peaks, dense forests blanketed in white, and the glistening Animus River meandering alongside the tracks. But as beautiful as the views were, the materials they had discovered in Robin's cellar beckoned their attention.

Ellen opened the journal of Arthur Lancelot Collins, the former manager of the Smuggler-Union mine. The leather-bound pages crackled as she turned them, revealing Collins's detailed defense of his controversial contract system for paying miners. Ellen shared with her friends:

"Collins staunchly defends his contract system, arguing against the $3.00 a day wage for an eight-hour day proposed by the Western Federation of Miners, or the WFM. He claims that a set wage would lead to laziness and inefficiency. 'If a man knows he will get the same wage whether he works hard or takes his time, he will tend toward laziness and wastefulness,' Collins writes."

Tanya and Sue listened intently, looking up from their own materials, each with a cup of hot cocoa.

Ellen continued, "Collins believed that paying miners based on the number of fathoms they harvested motivated them to be more productive. He argued that when miners were responsible for buying their own materials, they became more frugal and efficient. He further pointed out that the contract system allowed a worker to determine his own hours and be in charge of his own destiny. Collins criticized Vincent St. John and the WFM for trying to impose a set daily wage, calling it a form of coercion. He insisted that miners who disliked the contract system were free to seek employment elsewhere."

She looked up, meeting the eyes of her friends. "Collins seemed pretty adamant that his way was best for both the miners and the owners."

Tanya leaned forward. "But according to Charles Sumner's article in the *San Miguel Examiner*, the contract system was incredibly unfair. Sumner points out several flaws. For one, some areas of the mine were softer and easier to mine, so some workers could harvest more fathoms in the same time than others. Secondly, the width of veins varied, which means some miners spent more time harvesting the same length of a fathom."

Sue, always analytical, interjected, "So essentially, not every miner was on an equal playing field."

"Exactly," Tanya confirmed. "Sumner also mentions that miners had to provide their own supplies—powder, steel, candles—and often ended up owing more for these supplies than they earned from their contracts. He writes that many miners found themselves in debt at the end of the month. Additionally, the contracts often had quotas, and if these weren't met, the miners got paid nothing."

Ellen glanced down at Moseby, who seemed to be listening as intently as the rest of them. She sighed. "Collins counters that those who ended up in debt were lazy and predominantly Italian."

"Talk about racist," Tanya chided.

Sue shook her head. "No wonder this conflict was so difficult to resolve. Both sides were entrenched in their beliefs, seeing the situation from entirely different perspectives."

Ellen nodded. "Collins saw himself as a fair businessman, while the union saw him as exploiting the workers. Both sides had valid points, but neither seemed willing to see the other's view."

Tanya leaned back, a thoughtful expression on her face. "This must be why the spirits are restless. Buck Wells and Vincent St. John were both deeply involved in this conflict. It's no wonder they might still be haunting Robin's house, especially if they feel the past is unresolved."

"We still need to figure out who shot Arthur Collins," Sue pointed out.

"And why St. John murdered Barney," Ellen put in.

"And why it took seven years to find Barney's bones," Tanya added.

The train ride continued, offering more picturesque views of the San Juan Mountains. Snow sparkled like diamonds in the sunlight, and the river's icy waters mirrored the blue of the sky. Despite the beauty outside, the group's focus remained on the historical documents.

Ellen flipped through more pages of Collins's journal. "We need to understand what drove these men to such extremes. If we can uncover more about their motivations and the injustices they perceived, maybe we can find a way to help their spirits find peace."

Sue nodded. "We should keep reading and gather as much information as we can. If we know why these entities are angry, we might be able to address their concerns and hopefully stop the hauntings."

When they reached Silverton, they got off the train to explore the historic town for a couple of hours. Moseby was glad to stretch his legs as they toured two historic hotels, an art gallery, and several gift shops. They ate delicious sandwiches and charcuterie at the Lacey Rose Saloon.

"Brian would have loved this place," Ellen said of the saloon. "Maybe I'll bring him here sometime."

"We should all come back for a couples' retreat," Sue suggested.

Tanya rolled her eyes. "Good luck getting Dave to come. He never wants to do anything but work, and when he does finally agree to do something, he's grouchy the whole time."

"Is everything okay between you two?" Ellen asked gently.

Tanya frowned. "He just works constantly. He's a workaholic."

"Why doesn't he retire?" Sue asked. "It's not like he *has* to work."

"He loves it too much," Tanya explained. "He will never quit—not until he's dead."

"I guess it's the same for us and our work," Ellen pointed out. "I love our investigations and doubt I'll quit until I have to."

"But it's different with us," Tanya argued, tears of frustration falling down her face. "We go on two, maybe three, trips a year. Dave works long hours every single day. He rarely makes time to do things with me or the family, and when he finally does—ugh. Never mind. I don't mean to bring down the mood." Tanya wiped away her tears with her napkin.

Sue patted Tanya's hand. "Don't you worry about that. Have you told Dave how you feel?"

"Yes, but he thinks I'm needy. I don't think asking for his company once or twice a week is needy, do you?"

"Absolutely not," Ellen insisted. "But it sounds like you two just need to reconnect. Paul and I were going through this in the years before he died, and I regret that I didn't try harder to reconnect with him."

Unexpected tears formed in Ellen's eyes. She quickly wiped them away. "Sorry."

Sue patted her hand, too. "Well, who would have guessed that I would be the only one who has herself together."

The three friends laughed.

After lunch, they boarded a small mine train, the seats narrow and the engine emitting a nostalgic clatter. The guide, a middle-aged man with a grizzled beard and a hard hat, introduced himself as Joe. His voice was rich with the cadence of countless stories.

"Welcome to the Old Hundred Gold Mine, folks," Joe began. "We're about to journey deep into Galena Mountain, where miners once toiled to extract gold from the earth. Hold on tight!"

The train jerked to life, and they plunged into the cool darkness of the mine. The narrow tunnels seemed to close in around them, the walls damp and echoing with the sounds of the train. Lanterns along the walls cast eerie shadows, and the air was filled with the scent of earth and history.

Ellen leaned close to Moseby, who sniffed curiously at the air. "You okay, boy?"

Moseby gave a small bark, as if to say he was ready for the adventure.

As they traveled deeper, Joe pointed out various features of the mine. "These tunnels were all dug by hand, using picks and shovels. It was backbreaking work, often done in near darkness. The conditions were harsh, and the risk of cave-ins was a constant threat."

They stopped at a section where original mining equipment was still in place. Joe demonstrated how a pneumatic drill worked, the loud clatter reverberating through the tunnel. Ellen marveled at the sheer effort it must have taken to operate such machinery in these confined spaces.

"Imagine working with this all day," Sue whispered. "No wonder those miners were tough."

Joe continued, sharing tales of the miners' lives, "The miners faced many challenges. There was the constant danger of toxic gases, the physical toll of the labor, and the isolation. Many miners lived in shacks near the mine, cut off from their families for months at a time."

Tanya shook her head. "It's hard to imagine such a life."

Ellen nodded, feeling a deep respect for the miners who had endured such hardships. "They must have been incredibly resilient."

The train moved again, stopping at a cavern where Joe explained the gold extraction process. He showed them a stamp mill, an enormous machine used to crush ore to extract gold. The machinery roared to life, giving them a sense of the noise and vibration the miners endured daily.

"This mill was the heart of the operation," Joe said. "It was loud, dirty work, but it was the only way to separate the gold from the rock."

As they continued the tour, Ellen noticed Moseby's ears perk up. She bent down to pet him. "What is it, Moseby?"

Joe smiled. "Dogs were sometimes used in mines too, you know. They helped detect toxic gases and were loyal companions to the miners."

Ellen glanced at her friends. "Maybe Moseby would have made a good mine dog."

Sue chuckled. "As long as he didn't have to dig."

"Mo used to be a digger," Ellen said. "Thank goodness we were able to put a stop to that. For a while, my backyard looked like prairie dogs lived in it."

The train finally brought them back to the entrance, and they stepped out into the sunlight. Ellen felt a sense of awe and respect for the history they had just witnessed.

Joe tipped his hat. "Thank you for visiting the Old Hundred Gold Mine. I hope you've gained a deeper appreciation for the miners who worked here and the legacy they left behind."

Ellen, Tanya, and Sue thanked Joe, and as they walked away, Ellen looked back at the mine entrance. "That was incredible. I feel like we just stepped into another world."

Tanya nodded. "It's amazing to think about the lives those miners led. We've come a long way since then."

Sue sighed contentedly. "I'm just glad we could experience it from the comfort of a train, rather than the backbreaking way those miners did."

Ellen smiled, looking down at Moseby. "I think Moseby enjoyed it too. Right, boy?"

Moseby wagged his tail, clearly pleased with the adventure.

They eventually reboarded the Durango-Silverton train and looped back toward Durango. The friends took a reprieve from reading the old documents to enjoy cups of hot cocoa, the magnificent scenery, and their own conversation.

Tanya gazed out the window, her eyes wide with wonder. "You know, I read somewhere that this area has some of the most breathtaking views in the world. I think I finally believe it."

Sue smirked. "Yeah, it's beautiful, but I have to admit, my idea of a mountain adventure usually involves a spa at the base of it."

Ellen laughed, giving Moseby a gentle pat. "Sue, the way you talk, one would think you were a pioneer woman, blazing trails to the nearest hot tub."

"Hey," Sue shot back, "if the pioneers had had hot tubs, they would have used them. No shame in enjoying some modern comforts."

Tanya grinned. "Modern comforts? Like the 'sacrifice' you made yesterday to stay behind with Moseby?"

Sue rolled her eyes, but a smile tugged at her lips. "Look, I took one for the team. Moseby needed someone, and that someone happened to enjoy the scenery from a comfortable bench."

Ellen shook her head, chuckling. "I think Moseby enjoyed that 'hike' as much as you did."

Sue lifted her chin. "Do I need to remind you that Moseby and I had a very productive conversation with a local? While you two were playing mountain goats, we were getting insider info."

"True," Ellen said with a laugh. "You and Moseby made one dynamic duo yesterday."

Sue grinned. "He was the muscle, I was the brains. Isn't that right, Moseby?"

Mo looked up at Sue before nestling back into Ellen's lap.

Ellen sipped her tea. "It's amazing how two sides can see the same issue so differently. Collins thought he was being fair, while the miners felt exploited, like he was trying to get out of paying a decent wage."

Sue tapped her chin thoughtfully. "You know, this whole thing reminds me of the time I tried to negotiate a pay raise with my boss, back before the kids were born, when I was a CPA. My boss thought I was being unreasonable, and I thought he was being a cheapskate. In the end, we both compromised."

Tanya laughed. "Yeah, except in this case, the compromise involved strikes, violence, and murder. Kind of makes office politics seem tame."

Ellen smiled. "True. But it's a good reminder that history is never as black and white as it seems. There are always multiple perspectives."

Sue glanced out the window at the passing scenery. "Speaking of perspectives, can we all agree that mountain views are best enjoyed from a comfortable train seat?"

Ellen nodded vigorously. "Absolutely. Hiking is great, but this? This is luxury."

"Oh, guys." Tanya shook her head. "There's nothing like being in nature without anything between you and the beauty surrounding you. This train is fun but hiking rules. You girls are just too lazy."

"You sound like Collins," Ellen quipped.

"Soon, she'll be accusing us of being Italian," Sue added with mock reproach.

Ellen hugged Moseby closer, feeling a wave of contentment. "I think we've earned a bit of luxury after all the ghost-hunting and history-digging. Let's just enjoy the ride."

Sue raised her cup of cocoa in a mock toast. "To the comforts of modern travel and the mysteries of the past. May we solve them all without breaking a sweat."

Ellen laughed, clinking her own cup against Sue's. "Hear, hear!"

Tanya smiled, lifting her cup. "And to good friends who make the journey worthwhile."

Back in the rental car, Ellen glanced at her friends. "We've got a lot of work ahead of us. But I think we're getting closer to the heart of the matter. Let's head back to Robin's house and see what more we can uncover."

Tanya, Sue, and even little Moseby seemed ready for the challenge. They drove back through the snowy landscape, each pondering the past and its impact on the present. The mystery was far from solved, but with each new piece of information, they moved a step closer to finding the truth.

CHAPTER SIX

Conspiracy Theory

Ellen, Sue, and Tanya sat around the large, oak coffee table in Robin's game room, the afternoon sunlight streaming through the floor-to-ceiling windows that offered a breathtaking view of the snowy mountains and cascading falls. Moseby lay curled up on a thick rug by Ellen's feet, contentedly dozing.

Stacks of papers, old letters, and a dusty journal cluttered the table—the materials they had recovered from the cellar. The friends had been sifting through the historical documents for nearly an hour, engrossed in piecing together the enigmatic story of the mining conflicts.

Ellen leaned back on the sofa, massaging her temples as she stared at the pages of Arthur Lancelot Collins's journal. "It's just so hard to wrap my head around all of this," she said, sighing. "Every account we read seems to paint a different picture."

Sue, sipping her tea, nodded. "And they all contradict each other. One minute, St. John's a villain; the next, he's being framed. It's exhausting."

Tanya, who had been flipping through a book recommended by Leon, the Ouray librarian, suddenly snapped to attention. "Guys, you need to read this," she said, pushing the book toward Ellen. "It's by Maryjoy Martin, and it's pretty compelling."

Ellen took the book and began reading. After a few moments, she said, "Martin argues that St. John did not kill Barney because Barney was still very much alive at the time of the supposed murder. She provides evidence of a divorce decree signed by him two years after Barney's supposed death."

Sue leaned in, her interest piqued. "What? How is that even possible?"

Ellen continued, "The book claims that the Mine Owners' Association wanted to discredit the Western Federation of Miners, so they launched a campaign to blame recent unsolved deaths on the union: the murders of Barney, Barthell, and Mahoney. It says Barney disappeared from town but wasn't dead. Barthell, a union man, was shot by a non-union miner deputized by the MOA. And Mahoney, a non-unionized mine worker, never died—his death was fabricated by Eddie Curry, the anti-labor editor of the *Telluride Daily Journal*."

"That's wild," Tanya said, shaking her head. "So, the body they found seven years after Barney's supposed death wasn't Barney?"

Ellen shook her head. "According to Martin, the body was someone else entirely. Buck Wells, the manager and part owner of the Smuggler-Union Mine, was desperate to discredit Vincent St. John and the WFM. He managed to convince an entire town of St. John's guilt."

"Part owner?" Tanya repeated.

Sue leaned back, her brow furrowed in thought. "Wells orchestrated this whole thing to discredit the union? That's some serious manipulation."

"Yes," Ellen agreed, flipping to another page. "St. John was indicted and then acquitted for lack of evidence, but by then, Wells had done the damage he desired. Martin writes that Wells's deepest wish was to see St. John hang, but he settled for discrediting the union. She even suggests that Wells set off a bomb under his own bed to make himself appear a victim and add credibility to his political assault on the union."

"That's insane," Tanya muttered.

Ellen set the book down and looked at her friends. "It's a lot to take in. If Martin's right, then the entire narrative we've been following is a fabrication. It raises so many questions. If St. John didn't murder Barney, whose bones were found seven years later? And how do we know which sources among the many we've collected are to be believed?"

Sue sighed deeply, rubbing her eyes. "We need to cross-reference all these documents. Look for commonalities and contradictions. It's going to be a long night."

Tanya nodded in agreement. "We should also consider the motivations behind each source. Everyone had something to gain or lose. That might help us determine what's credible and what's not."

Ellen picked up Collins's journal again, flipping through the pages thoughtfully. "Collins was staunchly against the union, believing that the contract system was fairer than a daily wage. But his perspective was from a mine manager's point of view. He had everything to gain from keeping costs down."

"And the miners had everything to gain from a daily wage," Tanya added. "Guaranteed pay, for one."

Moseby stirred from his nap, stretching and yawning before looking up at Ellen. She scratched behind his ears, finding comfort in the simple, loyal presence of her dog amidst the chaos of conflicting histories.

"We need to keep an open mind," Ellen said finally. "Martin's book might offer a different perspective, but it doesn't mean it's the definitive truth. We need to keep digging, cross-referencing, and questioning everything."

Tanya leaned forward, a determined glint in her eyes. "Then let's get to work. We owe it to those miners to uncover the truth, whatever it may be."

"Not to mention peace of mind for Robin and her family," Sue added. "Those nightmares are relentless. I don't know how they can go to bed at night, knowing what's coming."

Ellen straightened her back. "I found a way to fight back." She proceeded to tell her friends about flying in her dream to take control of it. "You guys should try it and see if it works."

Sue raised her brows. "I've never flown in my dreams. I'll have to think of something else."

"I have an idea." Tanya lifted a finger. "If you can make Ken materialize for a romantic encounter, then you'll know it's just a dream."

Ellen guffawed.

"Now that's an idea I wouldn't mind trying," Sue said with a laugh. "Thanks, Tanya."

"Always glad to be helpful."

After the ladies had been at it for another half hour, Ellen said, "Why don't we organize all these papers and clippings by date and create a master timeline, noting any contradictions and commonalities?"

"There's an office upstairs with a conference table and a whiteboard," Tanya pointed out. "Why don't we take this project up there?"

"That's fine with me," Sue agreed, "but weren't we going out for dinner tonight? I'm getting hungry."

"Me, too." Tanya climbed to her feet. "Let's carry everything upstairs to the office and put the papers in order by year, just to get started. Then we can reward ourselves with dinner."

"Sounds like a plan," Ellen concurred.

The friends piled everything back into the dusty, plastic tub before carrying it upstairs to the office and began organizing the documents into eight piles ranging from 1901 to 1908. Outside, the sun dipped behind the mountains, shining lovely hues of pink and purple over the snowy landscape. Inside, however, Ellen, Sue, and Tanya were determined to shed light on the tangled web of history that had brought them here.

When they returned two hours later from a delicious dinner in Mountain Village at La Piazza Del Viaggello, the papers they'd sorted in the upstairs office lay in a scattered mess on the hardwood floor.

"Moseby didn't do this. He was with us," Ellen said defensively.

Moseby looked up at her from where he stood by her feet.

"We know Moseby didn't do this," Tanya said beneath her breath as she glanced around the room.

"Do these ghosts want our help or not?" Sue wondered with her hands on her hips.

"Let's sage and secure the room," Ellen suggested. "There may be some ghosts who want our help and others who want to hinder us from learning the truth."

The ladies set to work with a smudge sage stick and abalone shell, driving smoke from the office through a sliding glass door.

"All negative entities must leave this place," Sue declared. "Fly away, never to return."

Tanya poured a circle of salt around the perimeter of the room, while Ellen sprayed holy water into the air in every corner.

"Now, be sure to open and close our circle of protection every time you leave the room and return," Sue instructed. "Hopefully, this will keep any bad spirits from messing with our progress."

Only after the room was secure did they begin picking up the papers that had been strewn across the floor and putting them back into piles according to year. They counted 113 newspaper clippings, letters, and documents combined. Once they were sorted by year, the articles in each pile were then sorted by month and then date. Once they had eight piles of records in chronological order, they got to work making the master timeline on a whiteboard that took up one of the four walls in the room. Tanya stood at the whiteboard with an erasable marker and, at the top left corner of the board, wrote "1901."

Ellen lifted the journal of Arthur Collins into the air. "I just want to point out that this journal begins in the 1880s, but I don't think anything's relevant until Collins writes that he becomes manager of the Smuggler-Union Mine on September 1, 1899."

Tanya added that date and notation to the top of the board, directly above where she had written "1901."

Sue lifted the first record in the pile of papers from 1901. "This is a letter dated January 2, 1901, from Vincent St. John to Arthur Collins asking him to consider replacing his contract system with an eight-hour day at a $3 daily wage for each miner."

Tanya made the notation.

Ellen said, "Note that Collins defends his system in his journal on January 3rd and indicates that he replies with a rejection to St. John."

"Got it," Tanya replied.

Sue lifted two newspaper clippings. "The *Telluride Daily Journal* and the *San Miguel Examiner* both published articles on April 5, 1901, outlining the contract system versus the daily wage system. The *Journal* supported the contract system, and the *Examiner* seemed more sympathetic to the daily wage for workers."

Tanya made the note on the whiteboard.

"Collins has a journal entry dated April 26th," Ellen began, "describing trouble at Bullion Tunnel, where a non-union worker named John Stone was harassed at gunpoint by union men and told to leave town. Collins writes that he's going to appeal to the sheriff to deputize some citizens to protect others against the union."

"There's an article from the *Telluride Daily Journal* dated the next day," Sue said. "It basically says that Sheriff Downtain deputized Bill Jordan, Mel Robbins, Red Barclay, and Jack Hyde to protect non-union men."

Tanya added it to the whiteboard.

"Collins is angry in an entry on May 1st," Ellen said. "He writes that 350 men walked off the morning shift."

"Articles from both the *Telluride Daily Journal* and the *San Miguel Examiner* corroborate that," Sue announced. "The *Telluride Daily Journal* asserts that the Local 63 asked miners from other districts to stay away until a fair deal could be struck."

"I'll just put, 'Strike Begins,'" Tanya said as she wrote it on the board.

"There's another article in the *Telluride Daily Journal* dated May 6, 1901, in which Collins reminds the town of Telluride how important the mine is to their economy," Sue said. "And then in the *San Miguel Examiner* on the next day, St. John is quoted as saying, 'Out of 146 men on contract in April, 79 made over $3 per day. Sixty-seven made less, some as low as sixty-three cents—all before tools and materials are paid for.'"

Tanya wrote, "Collins defends the mine in *Telluride Daily Journal,* and St. John attacks contract system in *San Miguel Examiner.*"

"Oh, look.," Ellen began. "Here's an article from the *San Miguel Examiner* dated June 9, 1901, claiming that the new deputies terrorized union man Charley Carlson. They beat him up, kicked him on the ground, and fired shots in the dirt on either side of him."

Sue tilted her head. "Sounds like those new deputies got too big for their britches."

"Then in an entry dated June 17th," Ellen continued, "Collins wrote that he reopened the mine with 50 non-union men, letting it be known that he'd terminated the contract system, at least temporarily. He said that he planned to bring it back after the trouble died down."

"This article from the *San Miguel Examiner* claims that Collins refused to employ union men," Sue pointed out. "It's dated June 18th. Then, an article from the *Telluride Daily Journal* dated June 22nd says that stone mason William Julius Barney has been reported missing. It asks, 'Is this another victim of Local 63?'"

While giving Tanya a moment to catch up with her notations, Ellen remarked, "I wonder what provoked the *Telluride Daily Journal* to make such an accusation without any proof?"

"It certainly clouds the paper's credibility," Sue agreed, "though this article dated June 27th is from the *Denver Post*, and it, too, suggests foul play in Barney's disappearance."

"But it doesn't implicate anyone," Tanya pointed out. "That's the difference."

"Good point," Sue conceded. "And this article from the *Telluride Daily Journal* dated July 1st continues in the same vein, publishing Barney sightings leading up to his supposed murder. The editor, F. E. Curry, writes, 'Barney was taken to the railroad bridge where he was either killed, stunned by a blow, or in an unconscious condition from some dope previously administered, and was thrown into the river.'"

"There's no mention of who the witnesses were?" Tanya asked.

Sue shook her head. "I guess the media was about sensationalism, even back then."

"Here's a sensational story," Ellen chimed in. "This one's from the *San Miguel Examiner*, dated July 3, 1901. It says, 'Strikers gathered at Smith's store to convince non-strikers to leave the job. One union man, John Barthell, shouted to the mine guards and strike-breakers in his broken English that they were under arrest, though he had no authority to do so. The guards, led by deputized Bill "Shadagee" Jordan, fired at him, killing him. Then, bullets flew on both sides, as the union men were incensed over Barthell's senseless death. Vincent St. John was awakened with a call from a mine officer asking what they should do. The WFM president went up to the hill to supervise the release of the guards and non-union men, who'd been taken prisoner. The prisoners were marched out of town for the time being, for their own safety.'"

"I'll just write, 'Union man John Barthell killed by mine guards,'" Tanya said.

"But add a note that his murder was blamed on the union in the *Telluride Daily Journal* in a July 4th article," Sue advised.

"Got it," Tanya replied.

"Guys," Ellen said with her brows lifted. "Collins writes in an entry dated July 4th that he will petition the sheriff to make a formal request to the governor of Colorado to send troops to Telluride. Wow, this escalated fast."

"This article says that delegates were sent to investigate but found no need for troops," Sue pointed out. "It's from the *San Miguel Examiner*, dated July 5th. And then another article in the same paper on the next day says that the Western Federation of Miners and Arthur Collins agree to terms. Contracts will still be used, but a minimum of $3 per day will be paid to all workers."

Tanya wrinkled her nose. "That sounds worse for the mine owners. I wonder why they didn't just agree to the daily wage."

"Maybe pride," Sue put in.

"Collins writes in his journal that he will favor and promote non-union workers over the others and will continue to discourage the union by offering a reward for information about Barney's death, hoping to pin it on the union," Ellen said. "The entry is dated July 11th."

"An article from the *San Miguel Examiner* dated July 15th says that no one was prosecuted for Barthell's death, even though there were witnesses," Sue said. "The editor, Charles Sumner, points out the irony that the death of a non-union worker—W.J. Barney—has quickly become a priority to the manager of the Smuggler-Union Mine, while the death of a union worker—John Barthell—in which there were plenty of witnesses to make a case, has fallen to the wayside."

Ellen tapped a finger to her chin. "Interesting."

"Then it's October tenth before we hear anything new," Sue said. "This clipping from the *Telluride Daily Journal* accuses the union of foul play in the disappearance of non-union man John Mahoney. Buck Wells is quoted as saying that St. John is a menace."

A loud thud from downstairs caused all three ladies to jump in their seats.

Moseby whined.

"What was that?" Tanya whispered, her face as white as the board she'd been writing on.

"Maybe this is a good place to stop for the night," Ellen suggested. "Let's close the circle and go downstairs and investigate. Maybe something fell over outside."

Together, they closed the circle of protection and then crept out of the office, the floorboards creaking beneath their weight. Moseby led the way, his nose twitching as he sniffed the air. Ellen kept a tight grip on the banister as they descended the narrow staircase, her nerves on edge. The shadows seemed to shift and twist in the dim light, playing tricks on her eyes.

When they reached the bottom of the stairs, they paused, listening for any sound that might give them a clue as to what had caused the noise. The main floor was eerily quiet, the only sound the faint rustle of the wind outside.

"There," Sue whispered, pointing toward the living room.

Ellen's gaze followed Sue's finger, and she saw it: a large portrait that had been hanging over the mantle was now lying face down on the floor. The ornate frame was cracked in several places, and the glass that had once protected the painting was shattered, shards scattered across the wooden floor. Ellen scooped up Moseby to stop him from stepping on the broken glass.

Tanya gingerly plucked the portrait from the shards and turned it over, so they could be reminded of what the subject was. It was a stern-looking but attractive man in an old-fashioned military uniform, his eyes cold and piercing even through the layers of dust that had dulled the paint over the years.

"Remind me to call Robin in the morning and ask if she knows who the man is in that painting," Sue said.

Ellen swallowed hard. "This feels aggressive. Are y'all wearing your *gris gris* bags and tourmaline rings?"

"Of course," Tanya said. "You should know better than to ask."

Sue moved to the side table where they'd left the spritzer of holy water. She lightly sprayed the water around the room, muttering a prayer as she did so. "Just in case," she said, her tone light but her hands trembling slightly.

Ellen and Tanya joined in, adding more salt to the corners of the room, their movements methodical. The air seemed to grow heavier, as if the house itself was watching them, waiting.

"Should we clean up this mess tonight, or put it off to the morning?" Tanya wondered.

"I vote that we wait for the morning," Ellen said, rubbing her tired eyes.

Sue broke the tension with a wry smile. "Well, if I see Ken in my dreams tonight, this will have all been worth it."

Tanya chuckled softly, but Ellen only managed a half-smile. She hoped whatever ghost had caused this painting to fall was done acting out for the night.

They exchanged quiet goodnights, each retreating to her own room. Moseby followed Ellen, his tail wagging slightly as if to offer some small comfort. She closed the door behind her and leaned against it for a moment, letting out a slow breath.

As she climbed into bed, Ellen replayed the events of the night in her mind. The thud, the portrait, the restless spirits—it all felt like a warning, a sign that they were getting too close to something the ghosts didn't want them to uncover. She gave Brian a quick call with an update, omitting the frightening ordeal with the fallen painting. As comforting as it was to hear his voice, Ellen was still anxious after they'd said their goodbyes and ended the call.

But tiredness soon overtook her, and, as she drifted off to sleep, Ellen found herself hoping that the spirits would grant them a few hours of peace, at least until morning.

CHAPTER SEVEN

Fire

Ellen awoke with a jolt, the sound of a man's voice tearing her from the depths of an unsettling dream.

"The tram house is on fire. Quick!"

The urgency in his voice sent a shock of adrenaline through her, though she couldn't quite place where she was or who the man was. Before she could fully gather her thoughts, the man had grabbed a fire extinguisher and had sprayed the nearby flames, which seemed to do nothing to stop them from consuming everything in sight.

"This is pointless," he cried. "Let's get out of here!"

He rushed toward the door, leaving Ellen to scramble out of the cot she had been sleeping on.

She followed him in a daze, her heart pounding in her chest as she reached the door of the small shack. Flames danced menacingly outside, their heat pressing against the thin walls of the tram house. The man was already battling the fire, aiming the fire extinguisher at the base of the flames, but they roared back, relentless and wild. The small, wooden structure groaned under the assault.

Ellen stood beside him, staring blankly at the inferno, her mind still struggling to catch up. The man's frantic actions barely registered until he turned toward her, his face illuminated by the eerie glow of the fire.

"Let's get out of here and warn the others!" he shouted, his voice cutting through her fog of confusion.

Without thinking, Ellen followed him into the frigid, predawn darkness. The cold air slapped her awake as they stumbled away from the blazing tram house, the heat from the fire still licking at their backs. Her feet slipped on the steep mountain trail as she struggled to keep up with the man who had awakened her.

They hadn't gone far when they came upon another man, who was leading a horse and cart up the trail. The man beside Ellen shouted to him, "The tram house is on fire! We need to do something before it spreads to the tunnel!"

The second man's eyes widened in alarm. Without a word, he unhitched the cart from the horse and mounted the animal in one swift motion. "I'll warn the men," he said, his voice tight with urgency before spurring the horse into a gallop toward the distant smoke.

Ellen watched him disappear into the darkness, her breath coming in quick, panicked gasps. By now, more men had emerged from the nearby boarding house, their faces pale with fear as they ran toward the fire, clutching fire extinguishers and dragging a hose behind them. The scene felt surreal, like something out of a nightmare she couldn't wake up from.

One of the men, struggling with the hose, caught her eye.

"We need to blow up the Bullion Tunnel to stop the fire from getting into the mine," he shouted over the roar of the flames. "Follow me."

Ellen's heart skipped a beat. Blow up the tunnel? The words barely made sense to her in her disoriented state. "Who are you?" she managed to ask, her voice trembling.

"St. John," he replied quickly, not breaking stride.

The name sounded vaguely familiar to her, but there was no time for questions. Ellen stumbled after him, her legs moving on autopilot as they navigated through thick plumes of smoke and past flaming buildings. The acrid smell burned her throat and stung her eyes, but she forced herself to keep moving, her mind screaming that this couldn't be real.

St. John led her to a pipeline running along the ground, which he smashed open with a heavy sledgehammer. He quickly fixed the end of the hose to the broken pipe, ordering a man to hold it tight, and then he began spraying water onto the tunnel entrance. The water hissed and steamed as it hit the scorching ground, tamping just enough of the flames to make an opening at the mouth of the tunnel.

Ellen stood helplessly as two other men sprinted toward it, carrying sticks of dynamite. They disappeared into the tunnel, the darkness swallowing them whole. Moments later, they emerged, shouting, "Duck!"

Without hesitation, Ellen threw herself to the ground beside St. John, covering her head with her arms. The world shook as a deafening explosion tore through the air, followed by the thunderous sound of rocks collapsing. Dust and debris rained down around them as the mouth of the tunnel crumbled, sealing off the fire from the mine beyond.

For a few seconds, everything was silent except for the crackling of the fire.

Then, slowly, St. John got to his feet and extended a hand to Ellen. "Now let's get the men out and pray they're still alive," he said, his voice grim.

Ellen gasped and opened her eyes to find herself in bed with Moseby curled beside her. Through the window, she could see the moon bathing the snowy mountains in soft light. There was no sign of the ravaging flames that had haunted her nightmare.

Groaning, she closed her eyes and prayed again for a peaceful night's sleep.

Thursday morning, Ellen found Sue and Tanya sitting at the kitchen bar, the aroma of freshly brewed coffee mingling with the scent of toasted bagels. Robin's mountain home was bathed in sunlight, the expansive windows offering a breathtaking view of the snow-laced peaks and clear, blue sky. The setting should have been peaceful, but the weight of her nightmare hung heavily in the air.

"Good morning, sleepyhead," Sue said. "You missed all the fun. Tanya and I cleaned up the mess from last night."

"Oh, thank you. I'm sorry I wasn't up to help."

"No worries," Tanya said. "Sue and I were just telling each other about our dreams last night."

Sue took a sip of her coffee. "I spent the night dragging dead miners from the mine. It was awful. I could barely breathe or see, because the smoke was so thick. And their faces . . . I can't get their faces out of my mind."

Tanya spread cream cheese on a bagel. "I was with a group of miners trying to escape the deadly smoke in the mine. The hoist wasn't working, so we had to climb a narrow ladder for hundreds of feet through the manways. The smoke was so thick . . . we were coughing and gagging the entire time. I kept thinking we wouldn't make it."

Ellen shivered, the vivid images Tanya painted feeling all too real. She turned to Sue, "The dead miners you were retrieving . . . how had they died? Do you know?"

"Smoke inhalation," Sue replied. "We could barely breathe as we were pulling them out."

"Guys, I think we all dreamt about the same event last night." Ellen poured coffee into a mug. "St. John made an appearance in mine. He was there, trying to dampen the flames with a hose at the mouth of the Bullion Tunnel so two other guys could blow it up and stop the fire from spreading into the mine. He was a hero."

Sue leaned forward. "There's something going on here. These dreams . . . it feels like the spirits are trying to tell us something."

Ellen took a sip of her coffee. "Exactly. At first, I thought they were caught in a loop—and maybe they are. But last night felt like a message."

Tanya leaned back in her chair, her expression softening. "Why don't we get started on our timeline upstairs? We might find something that connects all of this. Then later, we can reward ourselves with a delicious lunch in town. I could use something to lift my spirits."

The suggestion brought a smile to Ellen's face. "Sounds like a plan," she agreed. "Let's see what we can dig up."

Since Moseby had just finished eating, Ellen took him outside for a short walk before returning indoors and meeting the others in the office upstairs. Her friends nearly pounced on her when she entered the room.

"You won't believe this," Tanya began.

Sue held two newspaper clippings in her hands. "A fire started in the tram house only two hundred feet from the Bullion Tunnel. It happened in the early morning of November 20, 1901."

Tanya nodded. "Twenty-three men died in the mine."

"According to the *San Miguel Examiner*, sixteen of them were union men," Sue added.

"And yet this article in the *Telluride Daily Journal*," Tanya picked up another newspaper clipping from the table, "implicates the union and St. John."

"That doesn't make sense," Ellen insisted. "Why would they jeopardize the lives of union men?"

"Exactly," Tanya agreed.

Ellen shook her head. "That editor . . . what was his name . . . Curry? He had it in for St. John. I wonder why."

"Who owned the *Telluride Daily Journal*?" Tanya wondered out loud.

Sue opened her laptop and got to work. After a few minutes, she said, "Charles F. Painter. He was also the first mayor of Telluride, and he owned an insurance company."

"And, as the mayor, wouldn't he be on the side of the worker?" Tanya wondered.

"Or the wealthy businessmen who elected him," Sue said without inflection.

"Well, as a politician," Ellen began, "he wasn't without an agenda. And as a business owner, he may have sided with the mine owners against the laborers. What about the *San Miguel Examiner*? Who owned it?"

"Hmm." Sue tapped at her keyboard. "Nothing's coming up."

Ellen opened to the index of one of the library books they'd received from Leon. "Okay, here we go. The *San Miguel Examiner* was owned by Charles Sumner and Charles Fluke. So, Sumner, the editor, was one of the owners. Let me see what I can find out about him. Okay, here we go. Maryjoy Martin writes favorably about him. He was born in Grand Junction, married his high school sweetheart, worked as a printer and then a reporter before moving to Telluride and establishing the *San Miguel Examiner* with Charles Fluke. She writes that although he was a strong Republican, his was one of the few papers at the time to pay union wages. She says he liked to give fair representation to all sides and to defend the innocent, even if it meant making powerful enemies."

"See, Tanya?" Sue teased. "Not all Republicans are bad."

"Oh, Sue. If I thought that, we wouldn't be friends."

"Are we to believe that sketch of him?" Ellen wondered.

"Well," Sue began, "it would certainly explain why he and Curry were at odds with each other in their reporting. In fact, this article in the *San Miguel Examiner* dated November 27th raises a lot of questions about the competence of mine manager Arthur Collins regarding the fire. It claims that because Collins promoted only non-union workers, the Smuggler bosses, less experienced than union workers, didn't know what to do. It goes on to say that the mine had the minimum number of fire extinguishers and hoses, and no one was trained in how to use them. It took Vincent St. John and other union workers from the Tomboy mine to stop the fire."

"Are you writing this down, Tanya?" Ellen asked anxiously. "This is important stuff."

"I'm on it," she said as she made the notations on the whiteboard.

Ellen opened Collins's journal, skimming to November 1901, to see if there was anything relevant recorded there. "Oh, this is interesting," she said after a while. "In an effort to subdue his negative public image after the fire, Collins writes that he agreed to a three-year contract with the union. He would pay a $3 daily wage for eight-hour shifts."

"Talk about trying to save face," Tanya said snidely.

"And the editor of the *Telluride Daily Journal* uses that outcome to throw suspicion on St. John," Sue pointed out.

"Oh, brother," Ellen complained. "Round and round they go."

Just then, Sue's phone rang. "Oh, it's Robin calling me back. Hi, Robin, you're on speaker."

"Good morning, ladies. I got your message about the painting. That's actually not the first time that's happened. Anyway, according to my uncle, it was in the cellar when his parents—my grandparents—inherited the log cabin decades ago, and his research led him to conclude that the man in the painting was a general in the National Guard named Buck Wells."

Ellen and her friends gawked at one another.

"Hello?" Robin asked.

"We're still here," Sue managed to say. "We're just in shock. We believe he's one of the ghosts haunting your house."

"*One* of the ghosts?" Robin echoed. "You think there's more than one?"

"Yes," Ellen chimed in, "and the other ghost, more likely than not, is the one who knocked down that painting."

Ellen and her friends spent the next hour recording the events of 1902 on their timeline. In January, the union boycotted the *Telluride Daily Jour-*

nal because the newspaper continued to disparage St. John and the Western Federation of Miners, and blue cards were distributed to union-friendly businesses to display in their windows, so union members knew which ones to support. In March, a battery of avalanches occurred, killing several people—the natural disasters General Gardner was quoted as saying were God's punishment on the union. Wesley Smith also disappeared in March, and Curry linked his disappearance to Barney's.

Then, in November, according to both the *San Miguel Examiner* and the *Telluride Daily Journal*, Arthur Collins was shot in the back while playing cards in the Smuggler-Union Office and House on the night of November 19, 1902.

"Wait a minute." Ellen's mind was racing. "That was exactly one year after the fire."

"The fire occurred on November 20th." Tanya pointed to what she had written on the whiteboard.

"The predawn hours of November 20th," Ellen corrected. "Essentially, the night of the 19th. After so many people blamed Collins for not training his bosses on what to do in a fire, don't you think it's too much of a coincidence that he was assassinated exactly one year later?"

They heard another thud from downstairs.

Moseby, who was curled on the rug by Ellen's feet, whined.

"What was that?" Tanya wondered.

"That could be confirmation from a spirit that we're on the right track," Ellen suggested.

"Or the wrong track," Sue pointed out.

"Well, whatever it was, let's leave it for now so we can figure this out," Ellen suggested. "Hopefully it's not more broken glass."

"All these newspaper articles blame St. John for the murder of Arthur Collins," Sue pointed out. "Not just the *Telluride Daily Journal*, but the *Ouray Herald* and the *Denver Post*, too. The *Herald* claimed that the union had an inner organized ring, like the Ku Klux Klan, and the *Denver Post* quotes St. John as having said, 'There are two or three more people in this place that ought to be removed, and then we'd get along alright.'"

"What?" Ellen stood up and leaned over the pile of papers on the table. "St. John said that?"

"I can't believe someone compared the union to the Ku Klux Klan," Tanya remarked with disdain.

"Wait, hold on." Sue was skimming another article. "This clipping from the *Rocky Mountain News* has a different quote from St. John. In this article, he says, 'The miners' unions all deplore the taking off of Mr. Collins and would never countenance violence upon anyone. I have never advocated the removal of anyone from Telluride, and such statements as attributed to me were never made.'"

"Wow," Tanya said, making the notation on the whiteboard.

"The *San Miguel Examiner* published an affidavit on November 29th," Ellen continued. "It was signed before the Justice of the Peace by four witnesses who were present during the interview with St. John by Polly Pry, the reporter who quoted him about wanting to get rid of a few more people in Telluride. They swore he made no such comment."

Tanya crossed her arms. "So that's proof that people were using the press to discredit St. John."

"Unless he was paying people off," Ellen pointed out, "but so far, sources have him as a poor miner, so I'm not sure how he could have pulled that off."

"There are only three documents remaining from 1902," Sue said. "One is a letter to Buck Wells from an inmate who called himself Crazy Miller saying that he knows where the bodies of Barney and Smith are."

"But I thought we established that those men weren't killed," Tanya objected.

"We did, but there you have it," Sue said. "It's dated December 10th."

"Crazy Miller was probably just trying to shorten his sentence by making a deal," Ellen theorized.

Tanya added it to the whiteboard.

Sue held up another paper. "This is a court record of an indictment before a grand jury on December 15, 1902, charging Vincent St. John with the murder of Arthur Collins, among other offenses."

"Oh, my gosh," Ellen groaned. "I can't believe it. They had no proof."

"And the last document of the year is a statement made by Buck Wells in the *Denver Post*, dated December 27th. It says, 'There is an element at Telluride that must be driven out before owners of mines will feel safe to continue operations.'"

All three ladies flinched at the sudden sound of another thud coming from downstairs. Moseby jumped to his feet and barked at the door.

"We'd better go and see what that was," Ellen said as she scooped Mo into her arms. "It's okay, Moseby-Mo."

When they reached the main floor, Ellen gasped.

"What on earth?" Tanya cried.

The dining room chairs lay strewn across the floor.

CHAPTER EIGHT

A Hunch

The road from Robin's house to the town of Telluride was less than a ten-minute ride winding through the mountains. The sky was clear blue—no more snowfall today—but the surrounding landscape was still covered with the soft, powdery stuff. Ellen kept her eyes on the scenery, her thoughts on the conversation she planned to have over lunch. Moseby sat comfortably on her lap, his head resting on her arm as he looked out the window. He was a calm presence, a little anchor in the flurry of thoughts swirling in her mind.

"Robin's uncle sure knew how to design a place," Sue said from behind the wheel, her tone admiring as she gazed out at the landscape. "That house is like living in a Christmas card."

"She may not be able to get us to leave," Tanya agreed from the front passenger's seat, adjusting the scarf around her neck. "But I'm glad we're heading into town. I'm craving something hot and savory."

"Cornerhouse Grille should do the trick." Ellen looked up from her phone. "It has amazing reviews and a good variety—though once I read 'lobster salad,' it didn't matter what else was on the menu."

"Oh, that sounds delicious," Sue agreed as she turned onto the main road.

"I thought you didn't like lobster," Tanya said to Ellen.

"Brian has made a convert of me."

Parking was easy this time of day, and soon they were making their way to the blue and white Victorian that housed the Cornerhouse Grille. The restaurant was a perfect blend of quaint and cozy, with its wooden floors, peeling paint, and a few antique mirrors reflecting the soft afternoon light.

Once seated, they ordered quickly—lobster salad for each of them and bowls of tomato basil soup to warm them up. As the server left, Ellen cleared her throat, glancing at her friends.

"I've been thinking about Arthur Collins," she began, keeping her voice low enough so only they could hear. "I still think it's odd that his assassination took place exactly one year after the fire near Bullion Tunnel. I can't believe it was a coincidence."

Sue raised an eyebrow. "You think Collins was murdered out of vengeance."

"Possibly," Ellen replied, her fingers idly tracing the edge of her napkin. "I wonder if it would be possible to find out the names of the 23 victims of that fire. Maybe we could see if any of their family members were still in the area when Collins was killed."

Tanya leaned in, her expression thoughtful. "We could check the Ouray Library again. Leon might be able to help us dig up those records. He seems to have a knack for finding things."

Sue grinned. "And here I thought librarians just shushed people and stamped books. Who knew they could be such detectives?"

The three women laughed, the tension of their conversation easing for a moment. Moseby, sensing the shift in mood, wagged his tail and gave a soft bark, as if joining in on the joke.

From Telluride the three friends drove a half hour north to Ouray to visit Leon at the library. Happy to help, he directed them to the microfiche and microform section, where he found a newspaper article from the *Salt Lake Tribune*.

With Moseby in his cloth pooch carrier, Ellen and her friends leaned over the machine to read the screen:

Telluride, Colo., Nov. 21. -- The developments today in the Smuggler-Union Mine disaster have not served to remove the doubt as to the number of the victims, and at a late hour tonight it seems unlikely that the exact number will be known for several hours. As yet the list remains the same as last night, twenty-two dead and one in a precarious condition from inhaling the deadly gas and smoke drawn into the mine from the burning buildings about the mouth of the Bullion Tunnel.

The mouth of the Bullion Tunnel, through which the Smuggler-Union mines are worked, is located not over fifty or sixty feet from the burned buildings. The smoke from the start seemed to be drawn to the mouth of the tunnel, and it encircled that point as if there were no other place of escape. This was due to the suction, as the air in the mine was warmer than that outside.

On account of this suction movement, the majority of mine and tunnel entrances have iron doors ready to lower in place at a minute's notice to stop smoke or fire. Unfortunately, the Bullion Tunnel did not possess one of these safeguards.

It appears that much of the stupefying effect of the fire was due to the flames in the converter house, which was saturated with oil and which emitted the darkest smoke imaginable.

The tunnel is situated about midway between the apex of the mine and the ninth level. It is an intermediate working tunnel. The seventh level is 1750 feet below the surface, and the ninth level, where between seventy-five and ninety miners were working when the fire occurred, is 2000 feet below the surface.

Seventeen of the twenty-two bodies recovered were found in the seventh level. The fire did not penetrate the mine workings, and the frightful loss of life was due entirely to smoke.

Many of the victims were married men and several left families. There is already talk of raising a relief fund for the widows and orphans, and it is quite likely that the State at large will be asked to assist the people of Telluride in caring for those who have so suddenly been bereft of their support.

The damage caused by the fire in the loss of buildings is estimated at $18,000, fully covered by insurance, but the mine will have to be closed down for at least a month.

The mine was originally owned by a company, of which John Porter of this city was the president and A. H. Fowler, secretary and treasurer. About two years ago the mine, with a number of others in the same locality, was absorbed by the New England Exploration Company, of which J. B. Lawrence is now the head and one of the principal stockholders. The New England Company is controlled by Boston capitalists.

Mr. Lawrence went to New York about a week ago. Arthur Collins, manager of the mine, is also absent on a trip to Mexico.

Names of the Victims:

Hugh O'Neil

Joe Nelson

Alex Fellman

John Ahone

Billy Jones

John Peterson

John Rals

Oberto Rafati

Thorvald Torkleson

John Nevala

Carey "Red" Barclay

Karl Maki

Gus Sundborg

Louis Borzaga

Autoine Anesi

Mark Zadra

William Merrifield

Matt Stark

Iva Sundstrom

August Kaanta

Emil Dahlstrom

Allen Hendrickson

William A. Graham

Frank Zadra

"So, Arthur Collins was on a trip to Mexico during the fire," Ellen noted.

"Do you think the families of the victims held him responsible for the missing iron door in the tunnel?" Tanya wondered.

"I would have," Sue put in. Then she said, "Wait a minute . . . Didn't Dante say his last name was Zadra? That's the last name of two of the victims listed here."

Ellen and Tanya leaned over Sue's shoulder to reread the list.

"You're right," Tanya gasped. "I wonder if they're his ancestors."

Sue turned to the librarian working at a computer desk behind them. "Leon, do you know of a way to cross-reference the last names of these victims with census records taken in the area?"

Leon cocked his head to the side. "We have a census database, but you'll have to enter each name one at a time to pull up any existing records. With twenty-four names, it could take a while."

"We'd better get started, then," Sue replied.

An hour later, the ladies gave up their census data search. They found plenty of surnames matching those of the fire victims living in the area between 1900 and 1910 but no way to rule any of them out as suspects in Collins's murder.

Ellen had a thought. "You know, the newspaper clippings we have at Robin's were curated by someone—by Collins, Wells, or Robin's uncle."

"What's your point?" Tanya asked.

"We should look for other articles published in the aftermaths of the fire and Collins's murder to see if we can find a connection between the two events."

"It's a worth a try," Sue conceded. "Leon? Any ideas for where we should start?"

Leon conducted a few searches on a nearby computer and then found microform and microfiche for them to view. Ellen and her friends poured over the articles, looking for any hint of a connection to support Ellen's hunch. Ellen was moved by stories of heroism performed by men who rushed into danger to save their comrades. One told of shift manager Thorvald Torkelson, already clear and safe when he rushed into the Bullion Tunnel, ninth level, to warn the others. He ran into shift boss Red Barclay, and they split the level between them—one going north, the other going south—to warn the men. Even though their lungs and eyes burned from the acrid smoke, they refused to turn back until the last man was found, and because the entrance to the tunnel was blocked, they rushed into the manways and climbed 265 feet to the seventh level, looking for another way out. Not all made it. Some died of carbon monoxide poisoning on the way up. Torkelson was one of them. One miner said Torkelson had saved his life but while climbing in the manway had said, "Look out below. I'll have to quit" before falling to his death. Similarly, Barclay was found dead near an ore chute where he had gone to warn the last men.

Hugh O'Neil, a seasoned foreman at the mine who'd been cut to shift boss after he joined the union, had volunteered to go down to the seventh level to warn the others. He'd gone down with another volunteer, young Joe Nelson, in the cage and told the engineer not to raise it until they signaled. A few minutes passed in deadly silence, so the engineer brought up the cage only to find both men prostrate. Nelson was dead, and O'Neil was barely holding on. Hugh was seventy-five and well-liked by all the men and was St. John's longtime friend and mentor. After working tirelessly for eight hours pulling out men, St. John went to sit with his dying friend.

Tears welled in Ellen's eyes. She glanced at her friends to see that they were similarly moved. She wiped her eyes with the back of her hand and scrolled further down the microform.

"Hold on," Sue said. "This looks like a possible lead. In his public letter of thanks to the mayor and citizens of Telluride for their help in saving lives during the disaster, Collins only mentioned one man by name—his trusted helper Thorvald Torkelson. The article speculates that the letter may not have been as well-received as Collins may have hoped—not because the people didn't admire Torkelson, but because many believed Hugh O'Neil deserved to be mentioned, too." Sue turned to her friends. "It was after this faux pas that Collins suddenly agreed to the union's terms of an eight-hour day and $3 daily wage."

Ellen bit her bottom lip. "Are you suggesting that the murder of Arthur Collins had something to do with this slight against the memory of Hugh O'Neil?"

"I don't know," Sue admitted. "Let's look at articles written in the aftermath of the shooting, to see if we can find anything to support that idea."

Not long into their search, Tanya spotted an article that filled in many of the gaps about the night of the murder. The article was from the *San Miguel Examiner*, dated December 26, 1902:

On the evening of the fatal gunshot, Arthur Collins's brother-in-law, Theodore Becker, along with Harold P. Smith, an assistant electrician, were returning from town toward the Smuggler residence. The two men, both employed by the Smuggler-Union Mine, were a little over a half mile from the residence, near the powder houses on the west side of Pandora, when they heard the shot. They remarked to one another that it was an unusual time for such a noise, noting it was too loud to be a mine blast and not quite sharp enough to be a rifle shot.

As they continued their walk along the railroad bed, they soon encountered a man carrying something long and narrow. Due to the gathering darkness, they did not see the figure until they were nearly upon him. The man stepped off the track to allow them to pass and then continued on his way. It wasn't until they reached the Smuggler residence and discovered Collins lying on the couch, bleeding profusely from a shotgun wound, that they realized the man they had passed was likely carrying a shotgun in a scabbard.

The two immediately contacted the sheriff's office, but no one coming from town reported seeing the mysterious man. Two miners descending from the Bullion Tunnel trail at the time of the shooting reported seeing a figure running out of the floodlight's glare near the house, seemingly holding what appeared to be a short-barrel or sawed-off shotgun.

Drs. Ochner, Sheldon, and Smith, along with surgical nurse Lena Strauss, were the first to arrive on the scene. Collins, though grievously wounded, managed to tell them that he had no idea who had attacked him or why anyone would want to shoot him. His injuries were severe; a lead shot had pierced his arm, four had struck his back, damaging his lungs, one had shredded his stomach and liver, and another had lacerated his kidney. The doctors administered opiates and moved him upstairs to his bed, where they performed a risky operation. Despite their efforts, they could only remove three of the seven pellets and held little hope for Collins's survival. Their goal was to keep him alive long enough to see his wife, Marguerite, one last time.

Marguerite and their two young sons were in Denver when they received word of the attack. A special train was arranged to bring her to her husband's side. She arrived in Telluride early the next morning, and Collins passed away shortly thereafter.

In response to the assassination, law enforcement quickly mobilized. Armed guards were placed on all roads and trails leading out of town, and a thorough search was conducted for the man with the sawed-off shotgun. The Smuggler property was combed for clues, and officers determined that the shooter had likely fired from behind a stump about fifteen feet from the porch. This location, obscured by a tall spruce tree, provided a direct line of sight to the window where Collins had been sitting. The next morning, a shotgun cartridge was discovered on a trail leading to the Pandora Mill, but no additional evidence has surfaced.

The case remains unsolved, leaving the community of Telluride with more questions than answers about the assassination of Arthur Collins.

"A single shooter," Ellen said. "He could have been hired by someone, I suppose."

Leon came over from where he had been conducting his own research and said, "Three different papers—the *Denver Post*, the *Telluride Daily Journal*, and the *San Miguel Examiner*—all published articles in the first half of January of 1903 about a man in custody who claimed to know who killed Arthur Collins. He claimed it was a man named Canun Siti shooting for someone else by the name of Evania Glavo. The articles report that Sheriff Rutan looked into it but found no such names on the payrolls." Then Leon lifted his hand in the air with a dramatic flair. "However, later in the month, the *San Miguel Examiner* published a follow-up article claiming that a C. Siti worked in the Revenue Mine, a few miles south of Ouray."

Ellen straightened her back. "Excellent work, Leon. Thank you so much."

Sue lifted her brows. "I wonder if Evania Glavo had any sort of connection to Hugh O'Neil."

"Or to any of the other fire victims," Ellen put in.

"Why in the world didn't the authorities look into that?" Tanya wondered. "The articles from Robin's bin focus on Vincent St. John as the primary suspect."

Sue shrugged. "I know. We last left off our timeline with St. John being indicted for Collins's murder by a grand jury."

Ellen sighed. "I think the anti-labor movement decided that the truth was less important than using Collins's death as an opportunity to bring down St. John and the union."

"And that anti-labor movement," Sue began, "was led by our very own Buck Wells."

Tanya nodded. "It's a sound theory. Why don't we go have dinner and then return to the house to ask the ghosts?"

CHAPTER NINE

Communing with Ghosts

Ellen sat at the head of the long, polished dining room table, her fingers drumming lightly on the dark wood as she surveyed the room. The soft crackle of the fire in the stone hearth offered a comforting backdrop to the otherwise tense atmosphere. Moseby lay curled up on the couch near the fire, his gentle snores a soothing contrast to the thickening suspense. After a delicious meal in town followed by a soak in Robin's hot tub, Ellen should have been feeling sleepy but was instead pulsing with anticipation.

Sue and Tanya were seated across from her, their expressions mirroring her own. The discovery of two ghostly presences—Vincent St. John and Buck Wells—had only deepened their resolve to uncover the truth.

The room was dimly lit, with only a few candles flickering on the table. Their paranormal investigative equipment—a combination of EMF meters, digital recorders, and cameras—was strategically placed around the room, quietly waiting to capture any sign of the spirits they believed were trapped within these walls.

Ellen leaned forward, her voice steady but soft, as she began the session. "Spirits of the other realm, we come in peace. I'm Ellen."

"I'm Sue."

"And I'm Tanya."

"We've come to help you move on," Sue added.

"Is Vincent St. John here with us tonight?" Ellen asked, her eyes locked on the others. "Please knock once for yes or twice for no."

They waited, the silence thick, until a single, distinct knock echoed through the room.

"One knock," Sue whispered. "That's a yes."

"Is Buck Wells here with us tonight?" Ellen continued. This time, the knock came quicker, as if the spirit was eager to communicate.

Ellen exchanged a glance with Tanya, whose face was pale in the candlelight. "Is Arthur Collins here with us tonight?"

The question hung in the air, and they held their breath, listening intently. Then, two sharp knocks broke the silence. Ellen frowned, her mind racing. Two knocks for no.

"And Hugh O'Neil?" Ellen asked, her voice dropping to a near whisper. The seconds ticked by, but the room remained eerily silent. No knocks. No response.

After a moment, Ellen stood and moved to the kitchen bar, retrieving two Mini Maglites from her bag. "Let's try something different," she suggested, setting the switch of the flashlights between on and off. She placed one on the kitchen bar and the other on the coffee table near the couch where Moseby was resting. His ears twitched slightly as she set it down.

"If Hugh O'Neil is here with us tonight," Ellen instructed, "please turn on the flashlight in the kitchen. If he's not here, please turn on the flashlight over there on the coffee table. All you have to do is tap it to make it turn on."

The seconds stretched into what felt like minutes, the tension in the room growing with each passing moment. Then, slowly, the flashlight on the coffee table flickered on, casting a faint glow over the sleeping dog.

"That's a no," Tanya whispered.

Sue exhaled sharply, a mix of relief and disappointment washing over her features. "What about Evania Glavo? Are you with us, Evania?"

The flashlight on the coffee table dimmed and went out, plunging that side of the room back into shadow.

"That could mean no," Tanya said softly, her eyes darting to Ellen. Before Ellen could respond, Tanya added, "If Evania is not among the spirits with us tonight, could someone please confirm by knocking once?"

The knock that followed was immediate and firm, leaving no room for doubt.

Ellen returned to her seat at the head of the table, her mind racing as she tried to piece together the fragments of information they had gathered.

"Are there more than two spirits here with us tonight?" Sue asked, but before she could finish, two knocks resonated through the room, cutting her off.

"So, only St. John and Wells are here," Tanya mused, tapping her fingers on the table as she stared at the flickering candlelight.

Ellen knew it was time to shift their approach. "Let's try the Ouija board," she suggested, her voice carrying a note of finality.

Sue and Tanya nodded in agreement, and the three of them lightly placed their fingers on the planchette that was at the center of the board, already laid out on the table.

After "opening" the board, Ellen took a deep breath. "Are the spirits of Vincent St. John and Buck Wells with us now?" she asked.

For a moment, nothing happened. Then, slowly, the planchette began to move to the top of the board: "YES."

Ellen's heart pounded in her chest, but she pressed on. "Is there a connection between the fire in the mine on November 20, 1901, and the assassination of Arthur Collins one year later?"

The planchette hesitated, then began to move again, spelling out letters that made little sense at first. Ellen's eyes widened as the words formed: G-O-B-A-C-K.

"Go back?" Tanya asked. "Go back where? Home? Do you want us to leave?"

The planchette began to move again, spelling: P-A-N-D-O-R-A.

"The ghost town?" Ellen wondered. But before Ellen had got out her question, the planchette continued: F-I-N-D-G-L-A-V-O.

Ellen stared at the board, the implications of the message sinking in. "Find Glavo?" she whispered, glancing at her friends.

"The ghost you saw," Sue began. "Maybe that was Evania Glavo, the man that the inmate said was responsible for Collins's shooting."

The planchette moved to "YES."

Tanya lifted her brows. "Looks like we're going back to Dante's Mountain Tours tomorrow. I'll go online and book us a time."

Ellen smiled with excitement at her friends. "This could be it, guys—our big break in the case."

"Now, don't get too excited," Tanya warned. "It might not amount to anything."

Sue waved a hand through the air. "That's the same thing I tell Tom when he tries to get me in the mood."

The three friends laughed as they "closed" the Ouija board.

"Are y'all too tired to work on the timeline for a while before we go to bed?" Ellen asked after blowing out the candles.

"I think I got a second wind," Sue said. "Tanya?"

"I'll make a pot of tea," she replied. "Anyone else want some?"

Ellen and Sue agreed that hot tea sounded perfect. While Tanya got the kettle boiling, Ellen and Sue put away their gear, and then the three friends and one dog went upstairs to the office.

Tanya stood at the whiteboard with her dry-erase marker. "We left off at the end of 1902 with St. John's indictment for the murder of Arthur Collins."

Sue lifted a newspaper clipping. "Here's an article from the *Telluride Daily Journal* dated April 15, 1903, reporting that a sawed-off shotgun was found hidden under a log in Royer Gulch. The two laborers who discovered it took it directly to Buck Wells, who believed it to be the weapon used in the assassination of Arthur Collins. Wells took the weapon to Sheriff Rutan and Deputy District Attorney Howe, who agreed."

As Tanya made a note, she said, "I wonder if they dusted it for fingerprints."

"I don't see any record of that," Ellen replied, "but here is a court record from the hearing before the grand jury. St. John's attorney, John H. Murphy, argued that the jury was illegally drawn. He stated that the sheriff was prejudiced and under the influence of the Mine Operators' Association, which caused him to summon men who shared his bias. In fact, several of the jurors selected for the grand jury had been heard by witnesses saying union members should be hanged. He pointed out that five of the men selected as jurors had signed the petition requesting the grand jury against St. John in the first place, which made them complaining witnesses—and you can't be a witness and a juror in the same case. The judge ended up ruling that the grand jury was not properly drawn, and the case was dismissed."

"How interesting," Tanya said as she made a note. "And what was the date of that record?"

"May 12, 1903," Ellen replied. "And here's another record from the 15th of May—a new complaint filed by Deputy District Attorney Howe on behalf of Buck Wells against St. John for the murder of Ben Burnham and Arthur Collins."

"Ben Burnham?" Tanya asked as she made the note.

Sue nodded. "He was killed at the same time John Barthell was killed, wasn't he? He was one of the deputized guards working for Collins."

"Yes," Ellen confirmed. "And several witnesses said that St. John wasn't even there yet when Burnham was shot, but there you go."

Sue lifted another clipping. "This article from the *Denver Times*, dated June 3, 1903, says, and I quote, 'The headquarters of the Western Union Federation of Miners was yesterday infested by an army of Pinkerton detectives who had discarded their stylish gray raiment and palmed themselves off as reporters. The miners could not guess why they were being so persistently besieged by reporters, as they knew of no news of importance which could be given out. Later in the afternoon, some of the officers, who almost knew the scent of Pinkerton, became wise, and then it was discovered that one Robert Meldrum, Sheriff Rutan's deputy, was hunting for Vincent St. John and Harry Jardine for the murder of Arthur Collins.'"

"Who was Harry Jardine?" Tanya asked as she made the note.

"It says here," Ellen, who had looked him up on her phone, began, "he was a socialist and union campaigner and the pressman for Local 63—the local unit of the WFM."

"I guess Wells thought they worked together on these murders," Tanya supposed as she took a sip of her tea.

"At any rate," Ellen continued, "according to this record, dated July 7, 1903, the case of the People versus Vincent St. John was stricken from the docket."

"But that did not restore harmony to the universe," Sue pointed out. "All these newspaper articles from September of that year talk about another strike, this one by the millmen. Apparently, the 8-hour workday that the Smuggler-Union had agreed to under Collins only applied to miners, not millmen, and the millmen walked off the job. One article says that over 700 men left Telluride to find work elsewhere. But Buck Wells refused to negotiate with the union. He's quoted as saying, 'No one will dictate how I operate this property. Now clear off. Don't bother me or my employees.' Then, he roped off the road to the mill and office and posted 'Do Not Trespass' signs. This article from the *San Miguel Examiner* further states that more mines were forced to close, putting miners out of work. And that very night, union man Sam Baral was shot outside of a union hangout—a saloon called the Silver Bell. *San Miguel Examiner* editor Sumner asks why the manager of the Smuggler-Union had no outcry for an investigation of this dead union man."

Tanya sighed. "It really is something how Wells became so obsessed with finding Barney's bones hoping to prove that he was murdered by St. John when other men who were killed meant nothing to him because they were union men."

"What makes it worse," Ellen began, "is that by January of 1904, Buck Wells convinced Governor Peabody to send the National Guard to Telluride and Wells himself was made a captain and given his own cavalry."

"And that's when the illegal deportations began," Sue chimed in. "The horrible nightmares we've been having."

Just then, the office door, which they'd left ajar, slammed shut. Moseby, who'd been curled up near Ellen's feet, jumped to all fours and began barking. Ellen and her friends exchanged worried glances.

"I think we made someone angry," Sue whispered with lifted brows.

"Want to bet on who?" Ellen whispered back.

With a shaky hand, Tanya returned the lid to her dry-erase marker. "Maybe we should sage ourselves and call it a night."

"I want to look over our footage first," Ellen objected. "But y'all go ahead, if you're ready to hit the hay."

Sometime later, Ellen jolted awake to the sound of a commotion outside, the noise piercing the stillness of the night. Her heart raced as she tried to make sense of the clattering and shouting. She glanced over at Moseby, who lifted his head from the foot of the bed, his ears perked up, alert but unalarmed.

"Stay, Moseby," Ellen whispered, sliding out from under the covers. She pulled on her robe and slippers, the cold seeping into her skin as she moved toward the window.

Her breath caught in her throat as she gazed at the spectacle below. Just beyond the glass, where Robin's patio and circular driveaway should have been, stood a bustling train station, illuminated by lanterns. Ellen's eyes widened in disbelief. The station was swarming with men—some in uniforms, others in rough work clothes. At the center of the gathering stood a massive Gatling gun, its wheels nearly as tall as she was.

Believing this to be a ghostly apparition, she hastened downstairs to the main floor, to get a closer look at the scene. Her pulse quickened as she scanned the faces in the crowd. Her gaze froze on a man standing near the gun, his stern features unmistakable. It was Buck Wells, the man from the portrait above Robin's hearth. As if sensing her stare, Buck turned and locked eyes with her through the window. A cold shiver ran down Ellen's spine.

Before she could react, Buck was at the front door, yanking it open and pulling her roughly into the night. The bitter cold licked at her exposed skin as she stumbled forward, her mind reeling.

"What are you doing?" she demanded, her voice trembling. "Let go of me!"

Buck's grip was ironclad as he pointed toward the train that had just pulled into the station, its whistle blaring through the mountains. The brakes hissed, and the train came to a stop with a final puff of steam.

"Those troublemakers think they're coming back," Buck said, his voice cold and flat. "But we're going to run them off again."

Ellen's heart pounded as she tried to comprehend his words. "What troublemakers?" she asked, her voice barely audible above the din of the gathering crowd.

"Union men," Buck spat, as if the words left a foul taste in his mouth. "Come on."

Ellen was dragged along behind him, her slippers sliding on the icy ground. The soldiers had already started moving, forcing men off the train and back onto it before they could even set foot on the platform. The union men, some visibly exhausted, offered little resistance as they were herded like cattle.

"You can't do this!" Ellen cried, struggling to keep up. "You've no right!"

Buck whirled around, his eyes blazing with a dangerous intensity. "I'm the law now, madam," he growled, the words dripping with menace. "Kindly step back."

Ellen recoiled, her fear momentarily overpowering her resolve. She glanced up at the train, her breath coming in quick, visible puffs. In one of the windows, she saw a man's face staring down at her, his eyes piercing and intense. Recognition jolted through her—it was Vincent St. John, the man from her dream about the fire and in the photographs she'd seen in her research.

As their eyes met, Vincent raised his hand and wrote something in the condensation on the window: *Find Glavo.*

Ellen's breath hitched as the words took shape, her mind racing to make sense of them. Then, she remembered that Glavo might be the ghost she saw at Pandora. Before she could react, the soldiers clambered back onto the train, followed by the ominous Gatling gun. The train's whistle screamed once more, and with a lurch, it began to pull away from the station, taking the men—and her last glimpse of Vincent St. John—into the darkness.

As the train disappeared into the night, Ellen was left standing alone in the freezing cold, the world around her eerily silent once more. She blinked, trying to clear her head. Was this a vision or a dream? She had been having these strange, vivid dreams since their arrival at Robin's mountain home, but this one felt different—too real, too tangible.

She took a deep breath, trying to ground herself in reality. There was only one way to be sure. Closing her eyes, Ellen willed herself to fly, to lift off the ground as she had done in her dreams before. But nothing happened. She was rooted to the spot, the cold seeping into her bones.

A deep sense of dread settled over her as she turned back toward the house. The door was still ajar, and the warm glow of the fire beckoned her inside. As she stepped into the entryway, she was met with the concerned faces of her friends.

"What were you doing out there?" Tanya asked, her voice laced with worry.

"You weren't walking Mo," Sue added, glancing at the little dog curled up on the couch. "He's here inside."

Ellen nodded, her thoughts a jumbled mess. "Buck Wells made me go out there," she explained, her voice trembling. "They were forcing the union men back on the train. It's just another stupid dream."

Tanya and Sue exchanged a worried glance.

"This is not a dream, Ellen," Sue said gently but firmly. "You're awake. We all are."

Ellen stared at her, confusion clouding her mind. Desperate to prove them wrong, she slapped her face hard, the sting sharp against her chilled skin. But the scenery remained unchanged—the warm, inviting interior of Robin's house, the tall Christmas tree, her friends' concerned expressions, and the cold night air still clinging to her.

Panic rising in her chest, Ellen rushed to the powder room and splashed cold water on her face, staring into the mirror as if the reflection might hold some clue. But the same face stared back at her, pale and wide-eyed. There was no escaping the truth.

She returned to the living room, her hands shaking as she scooped Moseby into her arms. The little dog licked her face, sensing her distress, but it did little to calm the storm of emotions raging inside her.

"What the heck just happened to me?" Ellen whispered, her voice barely audible. "Did you see the train station, too?"

Tanya and Sue shook their heads, their concern deepening. Tanya stepped closer, wrapping an arm around Ellen's shoulders. "You must have been sleepwalking," she said gently. "Come on, let's go back to bed, and we can talk about it in the morning."

Ellen nodded numbly, allowing Tanya to guide her back upstairs. As she climbed into bed with Moseby nestled against her, her entire body shuddered uncontrollably. The eerie dreams she'd been having since their arrival felt like a living hell, blurring the line between reality and nightmare.

As she lay there, staring at the ceiling, Ellen knew one thing for certain: They had to figure out how to help the ghosts move on, so Robin and her family could sleep peacefully again.

CHAPTER TEN

The Pandora Ghost

The sharp air of Telluride tickled Ellen's cheeks late Friday morning as she stepped out of the SUV, Moseby trotting alongside her on his leash. The little black dog's nose twitched as he sniffed the surroundings, probably noting the faint scent of pine mixed with the more familiar aroma of grilled food wafting from nearby restaurants.

"Ah, I'm starved," Tanya declared, rubbing her hands together. "How about we grab something at that little diner across the street?"

Ellen nodded, eyeing the cozy-looking building with its log cabin aesthetic. The afternoon sunlight glinted off the white peaks surrounding the town. But beneath the charm, Ellen couldn't shake the tension coiling in her chest. They had a job to do, and after lunch, it would be time to confront whatever spirit lingered in the forgotten corners of Pandora. Hopefully, that spirit was the ghost of Evania Glavo.

The three women and Moseby settled into a booth at the diner, ordering hearty sandwiches and bowls of steaming soup. As they ate, they discussed their plan for the day.

Tanya took a bite of her sandwich. "That vision you had the other day, Ellen—do you think it was Glavo?"

"I hope so." Ellen stroked Moseby's head, more focused on her thoughts than the food in front of her. "But it wasn't just a vision. He was there—solid for a moment, then gone. It was like he was caught between worlds, trying to reach out. I think he's desperate."

"It's too bad our equipment didn't pick up on anything that might offer more insight into this investigation," Sue said. "Just the two shadow figures—isn't that what you said, Ellen?"

"Fighting it out before the hearth," Ellen replied. "It's as if they've spent their afterlives in battle with one another."

"The same way they spent their lives," Tanya put in.

They finished lunch with a mix of determination and unease settling in their stomachs. Moseby curled up contentedly in his carrier, blissfully unaware of the task ahead. Soon, they met up with Dante outside his tour office, the sight of his burly frame and rugged Jeep giving them some confidence.

"Ready to head up?" Dante asked, adjusting his baseball cap.

"Ready as we'll ever be," Sue said with a flirtatious grin.

The journey up the mountain to Pandora was bumpy, the road twisting through dense forest and rocky terrain. The Jeep's tires crunched over gravel as they climbed higher, and Ellen couldn't help but think how isolated this ghost town must've been back in the early 1900s. Moseby sat perched on Ellen's lap in his cloth pooch carrier, his little ears twitching at every bump.

A few minutes into the ride, Ellen asked Dante, "Do you know anything about the two Zadras that died in the November 20, 1901 fire at the Smuggler-Union Mine?"

"Yes. They were cousins of my great-great-grandfather."

Ellen and her friends exchanged surprised glances.

Sue leaned toward Dante. "Ever hear of a man named Evania Glavo?"

"The Glavos and the Zadras are related, but I don't really know anything about Evania. Why?"

"We think he's our ghost," Ellen explained.

Finally, they arrived at the dilapidated remnants of Pandora. The once-bustling town had faded into weathered timbers and collapsed roofs. The chill of history clung to the ruins, and the shadows stretched long as the afternoon waned. They set up their equipment—EMF meters, thermal cameras, and the ghost box—and began their investigation.

At first, the air was thick with anticipation but devoid of any signs. Then, as Ellen adjusted a camera, a shimmery figure flickered at the edge of her vision. She turned sharply, and there it was—the ghost she had seen before, translucent and less defined this time, wearing what looked like tattered, old-fashioned clothes. The figure's face was obscured, but its presence was palpable. The ghost appeared to be trying to speak, but his words weren't audible.

Moseby whined at the end of his leash.

"Sue, turn on the ghost box," Ellen urged, her voice steady despite the chill racing down her spine.

The device crackled to life, hissing with bursts of static. Sue held her breath as the ghost box cycled through frequencies. For several long minutes, there was nothing but white noise. Then, a faint voice cut through the static: "I need moonlight."

Ellen's eyes widened. "Did you hear that?"

"I did," Tanya whispered, her hand clutched around her camera. "It was clear."

The ghost flickered, growing fainter, but before it vanished completely, the box crackled again. "Come back tonight."

The words sent a shiver through all of them. Moseby let out a low growl, staring intently at the spot where the figure had stood moments before. The apparition was gone, leaving only the ruins and the hum of the ghost box.

"Well, that was something," Dante muttered, his face pale. "Never heard anything like that before."

Ellen exchanged glances with Sue and Tanya. "Remember the Biltmore case? Zelda Fitzgerald's ghost wouldn't appear until the moon was full. Some spirits seem to draw power from moonlight, and it sounds like this one does, too."

Sue nodded slowly. "It's worth a shot. But we need to get back here tonight."

They all turned to Dante, who was shaking his head. "Ladies, I'm not sure it's safe. That road's bad enough in daylight, and going up after dark—well, it's risky. Plus, I have a family who expects me home in the evenings."

Sue leaned forward with a determined expression. "We'll pay you five hundred bucks for your trouble."

Dante hesitated for a moment, then grinned. "For five hundred bucks, you've got yourself a ride."

The cozy glow of the Smuggler-Union Restaurant enveloped Ellen, Sue, and Tanya as they sat at a small table near the fireplace. The smell of wood smoke mingled with the savory scent of their lamb sausage gyros. Ellen, who had Moseby in his cloth pooch carrier, took a bite, savoring the seasoned meat wrapped in warm pita, and exchanged an appreciative look with her friends.

"Now this," Sue said, waving a piece of gyro in the air, "is the real paranormal experience. Who knew a lamb sausage could be so divine?"

Tanya chuckled as she reached for her wine. "I was expecting a rustic mining town vibe, but this place could win a food critic's heart. Though I doubt any of those ghosts in Pandora ever had a meal like this."

"Maybe that's why they're so cranky," Ellen suggested, wiping her mouth with a napkin. "They're stuck in an afterlife of cornbread and hardtack. I'd haunt people too if that was my eternity."

Sue grinned mischievously. "St. John probably thinks we're management spies from the Mine Owners' Association, here to sabotage his revolution."

Tanya shook her head. "I still can't believe they made Wells a captain in the National Guard. Can you imagine the nerve? It's like promoting the fox to guard the henhouse."

"Oh, the irony," Ellen said, shaking her head. "The man who kept miners under his thumb becomes the one armed to the teeth, enforcing the law during a labor dispute."

Tanya lifted her brows. "Ah yes, Captain Corruption, protector of profits and crusher of proletarians! All hail the captain!" She made a little bow with palms down, and they all laughed.

"Now, don't start sounding like a communist, Tanya," Sue teased.

"Socialism and communism aren't the same thing," Tanya pointed out.

Ellen, sensing an argument coming on, said playfully, "I must admit, I wouldn't mind seeing the wine cellars of the mining barons from those days. Maybe we should ask Wells where they stashed the good stuff and if there's any left near Robin's house."

"Let's work those questions in during our next séance," Sue agreed. Then, after finishing the last of her wine, she added, "I bet our husbands are eating pizza or microwave dinners right about now."

Tanya nodded. "Dave never stops working long enough to cook or to pick something up, so, knowing him, he either ordered food or ate something from the freezer."

"Brian probably experimented again and *then* ordered food," Ellen said. "I almost feel guilty that we've got lamb sausage and ghostly adventures."

"Almost guilty, but not quite," Tanya said with a mischievous grin.

"Exactly," Sue said, raising her glass. "Here's to lamb gyros, haunted mines, and never letting a ghost ruin our fun."

They clinked glasses, reveling in the shared humor that was as comforting as the meal itself. As the light outside dimmed, Ellen felt a twinge of nervous anticipation, knowing that soon they'd be back in Pandora, with Dante leading the way.

But for now, with the fire crackling and laughter filling the room, the night's darker prospects seemed a little less daunting.

The clock struck seven as Ellen, Sue, and Tanya walked into Dante's tour office, Moseby trotting at their heels. The darkness outside was nearly complete, save for the gleam of the nearly full moon hanging low over the mountains. The temperature had dropped sharply, making the night feel more sinister. Ellen zipped her coat higher and adjusted Moseby's sweater as they greeted Dante.

"Alright, you brave souls," Dante said, though his jovial tone was tinged with nerves. "You sure you want to do this?"

"We wouldn't be here if we weren't," Ellen replied, her voice calm. She was no stranger to fear, but the stakes tonight felt higher. The possibility of contacting Evania Glavo's ghost was too important to pass up.

They piled into the Jeep, the headlights cutting through the night as they ascended the treacherous road to Pandora. The vehicle rocked and jolted over the rugged trail, and the oppressive silence of the forest pressed in from all sides. Moseby huddled close to Ellen, his little body tense in his carrier.

Once they arrived at the ghost town, the ruins looked even more eerie under the thin light of the moon. Shadows danced over the crumbling buildings, and the wind whispered through gaps in the old wood. The team quickly set up their equipment, fingers stiff from the cold.

Ellen took a deep breath and stepped forward. "Evania Glavo, my name is Ellen, and these are my friends, Sue and Tanya. We're here to help you move on. We need to know what happened to you. Please show yourself."

The air felt heavier, as if time itself had slowed. Then, as if summoned by Ellen's words, a shape coalesced in front of them. The figure Ellen had seen before appeared, his form solidifying until he looked nearly flesh and blood. He was a short man with dark hair and an olive complexion, dressed in raggedy, old-fashioned clothes. His eyes gleamed with a mix of sorrow and bitterness.

Sue gasped. "He's so clear!"

"Are you Evania Glavo?" Ellen asked as Moseby whined in his carrier against her.

"Yes," he replied, his accent thick.

Ellen and her friends exchanged looks of excitement.

"What happened to you?" Sue asked. "Are you stuck?"

Evania's eyes fixed on them. His thick accent was sometimes hard to understand, but his words carried the weight of decades of anguish. "I was murdered," he said, his voice trembling with years-old pain. "My body . . . defiled. I cannot rest."

Ellen took a cautious step forward. "We need to know more, Evania. Why were you killed? Where are your remains?"

Evania's gaze darkened. "I hired a man . . . to kill Arthur Collins—the manager of the mine. He deserved it . . . for the deaths of my cousins and so many others in that fire at the mine. The men killed because of him . . . my family demanded justice."

Tanya's voice was barely a whisper. "So, you had him assassinated?"

Evania nodded. "Collins had to die . . . but I couldn't do it myself. My friend, Canun Siti, did it . . . for money. We timed it . . . the anniversary of my cousins' deaths. After, Canun left . . . never seen again. But I . . . I confessed to Buck Wells four years later."

Ellen leaned in closer, hanging on every word. "What happened then?"

"Wells betrayed me," Evania spat, his anger palpable. "Locked me in his cellar . . . ordered someone to kill me. He shot me . . . hid my body . . . broke me apart. My bones . . . defiled."

The ghost's form shimmered, growing more transparent, his sorrow giving way to something darker. "Before I died, I cursed Buck Wells. Invoked *malocchio. Possa la tua anima essere divisa come tu dividi le mie ossa. Non troverai pace finché tutto non sarà riunito, finché la terra non prenderà ciò che hai disperso e la verità non sarà rivelata.*"

The ladies exchanged looks of confusion.

"What does that mean?" Ellen asked.

The ghost began to flicker and become more transparent.

"Where are you buried?" Sue asked, desperation creeping into her voice.

Evania shook his head, his figure fading. "I don't know."

The ghost flickered, then vanished completely, leaving them in the biting cold with more questions than answers. Ellen's heart pounded as the reality of their situation sank in. They needed to find out what Glavo said, to understand the curse, if they had any hope of breaking it.

She replayed the audio captured on her EVP recorder and fast-forwarded to the right place: "Before I died, I cursed Buck Wells. Invoked *malocchio. Possa la tua anima essere divisa come tu dividi le mie ossa. Non troverai pace finché tutto non sarà riunito, finché la terra non prenderà ciò che hai disperso e la verità non sarà rivelata.*"

"Is that Italian?" Ellen asked Tanya.

"I think so. It's not French or Spanish."

"My grandfather knows Italian," Dante said suddenly. "I could call him, and we could play it to him over the phone."

"Would you do that?" Tanya asked excitedly. "That would be so helpful."

Dante took his phone from his back jean pocket and made the call. "Nonno, it's Dante. Fine, fine . . . Nonno, I need your help. It's something in Italian. Will you listen and tell me what it means? . . . I know, I should have learned . . . Okay, thank you. Here it goes."

Ellen replayed the audio.

Dante put the phone on speaker. "What does it mean, Nonno?"

A frail-sounding voice with a thick accent came over the phone. "He said, 'May your soul be divided as you divide my bones. May you know no peace until all is made whole again, until the ground takes what you have scattered and the truth is laid bare.' He invoked *malocchio*—the evil eye. You know about the evil eye, Dante." The sound of the old man spitting three times came over the speaker.

"Yes. Thank you, Nonno. Let me call you back." He ended the call and said, "The evil eye is an old Italian curse."

"Do you know how to break it?" Sue asked eagerly.

"The answer is in the curse," Dante replied. "The evil eye won't be lifted until Glavo's remains are united and properly buried."

Ellen exchanged an anxious glance with her friends. "How on earth can we find his remains?"

"That's the million-dollar question," Sue said with a sigh.

"The evil eye is usually invoked when someone is jealous or envious of someone," Dante explained, "but it can be used for any powerful emotion, I suppose."

"My husband's family believed in the evil eye," Tanya said. "They were from Mexico. His mother used to say you should always kiss a baby and spit three times, just to be safe."

"My mother said something similar," Dante said with a nod. "Babies are the most vulnerable to the curse. In my family, people give newborns a necklace with a horn and a medal of St. Christopher for protection."

"My mother-in-law wore a horn necklace, too," Tanya said. "And she put dried chilis over her kitchen stove."

"Because they look like horns," Dante said, nodding again. "I grew up with protections against *malocchio*, but what happened here tonight—I've never seen anything like it. You ladies are brave. Let me help you pack up this equipment."

"We do it to help the dead find peace," Ellen said solemnly as she grabbed one of the cameras.

"And to help the living," Sue added.

"Let's get out of here," Dante said as they loaded the last of the equipment into the Jeep.

While they rode back down the mountain in tense silence, Ellen's mind raced. Finding Evania's remains could take days, weeks, or even longer. And without those remains, they might be dealing with a dangerous spirit capable of more than just curses.

Ellen glanced at her friends, knowing they were thinking the same thing. They'd faced tough cases before, but this one might be the hardest yet. If Evania couldn't guide them, how would they ever find his bones and bring him and Buck Wells the peace they both needed? And what about St. John? How did his ghost figure into all of this?

The mystery was far from over.

Back at Robin's house, the three friends decided to do a little more work on their timeline before heading to bed. Tanya added Canun Siti and Evania Glavo's names to the whiteboard as the gunman and mastermind of Arthur Collins's assassination. She also made a note that sometime in 1906, Glavo confessed to Wells, who then had him killed and his bones defiled. She put a big question mark and wrote, "Where are Glavo's bones?"

Sue lifted another newspaper clipping into the air. "This article from the *Telluride Daily Journal* dated February 21, 1904, says that Major Hill turned over command of martial law to Captain Buck Wells."

"It astounds me," Tanya said as she made a note, "that such a thing could happen in the first place."

"Captain Wells didn't waste any time putting his power to use," Ellen remarked. "An article from *San Miguel Examiner* dated February 24, 1904, says that Wells ordered a restaurant that catered to union men to shut down. It was called the Cosmopolitan, and when its owner, Baldwin, protested, Wells had him arrested and deported."

"Martial law at its finest," Sue said with a snort. Then leaning over another article, she added, "Actually, it gets worse. Wells ordered his men to build a stone structure he dubbed 'Fort Peabody' on the peak overlooking Imogene Pass—the only way back into town back then. He ordered his men to shoot any of the deported men trying to return to Telluride to their families."

"How awful," Tanya said as she added it to the whiteboard. "Unbelievable."

Ellen lifted a finger. "It gets even worse. According to this article, Wells had 34 strikers arrested for vagrancy."

"Isn't that illegal?" Sue wondered.

"Yes," Tanya confirmed. "I don't know how he got away with it."

"Well, at first he didn't," Ellen said, holding up another article. "This one from March 11, 1904, says that 52 plaintiffs filed a restraining order against Wells and that Governor Peabody relieved him of his duties."

"Thank God," Tanya said, making the note.

"Hold on," Sue said, sitting up straight. "That didn't last long. Buck and his cohorts held a meeting, assembling a mob of 50 men who broke into homes in the middle of night, holding union men at gunpoint barefoot in the snow and ice—"

"Our dreams," Tanya interrupted.

"Yes," Sue confirmed. "He forced 65 men to leave or be hanged. And then—get this—Governor Peabody reinstated martial law and Adjutant General Sherman Bell authorized Wells to resume with his troops! Bell even brought a Gatling gun to show he meant business."

"But Wells was the troublemaker," Tanya objected. "This makes no sense."

Sue added, "Here's a statement from Wells issued on April 5, 1904. He writes: 'We do not propose to enter into negotiations with the Western Federation of Miners. We do not recognize a union in Telluride. There is no strike in Telluride. All our mines are working with a full force of men, and we do not know what kind of settlement can be made. With us, there is absolutely nothing to settle.'"

Ellen and Tanya exchanged looks of astonishment.

"Oh, and look at this," Sue held up another clipping. "This is your vision, Ellen. Dated April 8, 1904, it says that Wells organized soldiers with General Bell and his Gatling gun to meet the train returning with the deportees. He and his men searched and bullied the union men and marched them back onto the train, escorting them to Dallas Divide, where they were forced off and made to walk in the icy darkness back to Ridgeway."

Ellen shuddered. "Wells was a monster."

They heard a loud thud downstairs. Moseby ran from the room, barking.

"Moseby, wait!" Ellen jumped to her feet and followed him downstairs.

Finding no sign of her dog on the main level, she went down to the game room, where she found him barking at the cellar door, which was ajar. She scooped her dog up and returned to the main floor, where Tanya and Sue were waiting, their faces as pale as a sheet.

"What?" Ellen asked.

Her friends pointed with shaky fingers at the painting on the mantle. Thrust through the canvas in the heart of Buck Wells was a steak knife.

Ellen gasped and hugged Moseby closer to her. "Do you think St. John did that?"

Tanya shrugged. "I didn't think he was the violent type, but people sometimes change after death."

Ellen thought of the shade in Santa Fe and shuddered.

"Maybe we should call it a night," Sue suggested. "Be sure to put extra salt around your beds."

"Good night," they said to one another.

Ellen took Moseby outside on his leash one more time to do his business before bed, feeling safer in the cold, dark night than she did in Robin's house.

Ellen awoke with a jolt, her heart hammering in her chest. Her gaze darted around what was Sophie's bedroom, the darkness pressing in from all corners. The only sound was the soft hum of the house at rest.

She let out a shaky breath, reaching out instinctively for Moseby, who was usually curled up by her side. But the bed was empty.

Before she could call out to him, an icy draft swept through the room. The temperature plummeted, and her breath misted in the frigid air. She shivered violently, pulling the blanket tighter around her shoulders.

Then, she saw him.

A shadowy figure materialized at the foot of her bed, the pale outline of a man wearing an outdated military uniform. His face was gaunt, his eyes hollow and dark, glinting with malice. Ellen's breath hitched as the ghost's voice slithered through the silence, cold and unforgiving. As he neared her, she had a shock. He looked exactly like the man in the painting over Robin's fireplace.

"Evania," he hissed, his voice rough like gravel. "You must come."

Ellen's heart thudded in her ears. "Buck Wells? Is that you?"

"It's for your own protection." The spirit's voice deepened into a menacing growl as he gestured toward the door. "There are others who know what you've done."

Terror gripped her, and Ellen found herself rising from the bed, her legs moving of their own accord. It was as if invisible hands forced her forward, pulling her out of the room and down the hallway. She tried to scream, to fight, but her throat felt paralyzed, her limbs leaden.

She was marched down the two flights of stairs, each step echoing eerily in the dead of night. As she descended to the game room, the shadows seemed to stretch and twist into grotesque shapes, closing in around her. The ghost loomed at her side, his bony fingers brushing against her arm, compelling her forward into the cellar.

The air in the cellar was thick and damp, with the scent of mold and decay hanging heavily. Ellen's feet shuffled across the cold dirt floor, taking her toward a decrepit wooden door tucked away in the far corner. The door creaked open on rusted hinges, revealing a smaller, darker room beyond.

"Stay in there," the ghost commanded, his voice tightening with urgency. "It's for your own good, Evania. Stay! They want Collins vindicated."

Confusion and fear clouded her thoughts. He had the wrong person. She wasn't Evania. Her mind reeled as she stumbled into the tiny room, her back pressed against the rough wall. The ghost's face twisted in anger, his features warping in the dim light. Then, with a thunderous crash, the door slammed shut, trapping her in the darkness.

Ellen squeezed her eyes shut, willing herself to wake up from this nightmare. Her breath came in short gasps as panic clawed at her chest. But then, just as suddenly as it had started, the cold and darkness vanished.

She was back in Sophie's room.

Her eyes flew open, her hands clutching the quilt. Everything seemed normal—the moonlight seeping through the curtains, the gentle rustling of the trees outside. It had been a dream—a nightmare. But it had felt so real. Her heart still pounded loudly as she quickly glanced around, searching for Moseby.

But he wasn't there.

"Moseby?" she whispered, her voice trembling.

Panic flared as she slipped out of bed, trying to keep quiet so as not to wake Tanya, who was in the other guest room. She searched every corner of the upstairs floor, but there was no sign of him. Her anxiety grew as she hurried down the stairs to the main level, her steps cautious and soundless.

No Moseby there, either.

Fear gnawed at her as she made her way down to the lower level. As soon as she reached the bottom of the stairs, she noticed the door to the cellar was ajar, a dark void beyond it.

"Moseby?" she called softly, her voice wavering.

A faint whimper reached her ears, coming from deep within the cellar. Dread washed over her, but she couldn't leave him down there. She took a deep breath and descended into the darkness, her hands outstretched to feel her way.

She heard the whimper again, closer now. With trembling fingers, she found the old, wooden door and pushed it open. "Moseby?" she called, her voice quivering. There was a rustling sound in the corner of the tiny room. Blindly, she reached out, and her hands found his warm fur. Relief surged through her as she scooped him into her arms.

But before she could turn to leave, the door slammed shut behind her.

It was exactly like the dream.

Her pulse raced as she tried the door. It was locked tight. She pounded on it, yelling for Sue, for Tanya, for anyone, but her cries echoed uselessly in the silence. No one came. No one heard. Despair choked her, the air in the room stifling and oppressive. Eventually, she slumped down to the dirt floor, clutching Moseby close, tears slipping down her cheeks as she rocked back and forth.

At some point, exhaustion overtook her, and she dozed off, still holding Moseby. But a harsh voice soon roused her from the uneasy slumber.

"Come on, Glavo," a gruff voice barked, a light flashing in her face. She blinked against the sudden brightness, disoriented.

A man she didn't recognize loomed above her, his expression hard and merciless. He grabbed her by the arm, yanking her to her feet.

"No! Let me go!" she cried, struggling against his grip.

The man's eyes narrowed as he raised a revolver and struck her across the back of the head. The pain exploded in her skull, and everything went black.

When she came to, Moseby's soft whines filled her ears. A light shone in her face again, and she heard a familiar voice.

"Moseby? Ellen?" Tanya's worried tone pierced the fog in her mind.

"Oh my God, yes, it's us," Ellen croaked from inside the small cellar closet. She dragged herself to her feet with Mo in her arms, relief flooding her. "What a terrible night."

"What happened?" Sue asked from the top of the stairs. "What are you doing down there?"

"I'm not sure how much was a dream and how much was real," Ellen groaned. "I don't think I slept a wink."

"Do you need to go back to bed?" Tanya asked.

"No way," Ellen said, following Tanya up the steps. "I don't think I can sleep in this house again."

<u>CHAPTER ELEVEN</u>

Buck Wells

Saturday morning, Moseby ate his food on the kitchen floor while the humans enjoyed coffee and bagels at the kitchen bar in Robin's stunning mountain home. It was another cloudless sky with a bright sun making the snow sparkle like diamonds beneath its cheery rays. As Ellen took Mo outside to do his business, she inhaled a slow, deep breath and tried to enjoy the grandeur around her, hoping to erase the memory of the troubling night. She'd been serious when she'd said she would not sleep here again. She didn't know how Robin and her family had lasted for four months. Ellen was determined to book a hotel in Telluride for the remainder of their investigation.

She removed Moseby's leash, and he followed her as she carried her coffee to the upstairs office, where her friends were already busy combing through the remaining materials.

Tanya handed her the library book written by Maryjoy Martin. "We thought we'd make a more comprehensive sketch of Buck Wells before carrying on with the timeline, to get a better sense of his character. Check out these pages in Martin's book."

According to Martin, Buck Wells was born Bulkely Wells in Chicago on March 10, 1872, to a businessman and homemaker. He was educated at Roxbury Latin School and Harvard. Already born into privilege, his career took off when he married Grace Daniels Livermore, the daughter of a wealthy colonel in Boston who owned shares in the Smuggler-Union Mine. Wells became a 32nd degree Mason and dazzled everyone with his good looks with his beautiful wife on his arm. He loved to hunt bear, deer, and fowl and loved to shoot competitively whenever he had the chance. He also enjoyed playing polo and racing fine horses, an endeavor supported by his wife's wealth. One of his favorite activities was to "rough it" as he camped in the woods in splendor with fine china, silver service, and the most expensive champagne.

Martin wrote that after Buck Wells took on the position of manager at the Smuggler-Union Mine, it wasn't long before he was deputized and made a captain and, soon after, a general in the National Guard. He was a member of the executive board of the Mine Owners' Association and had the ear of Governor Peabody, the city sheriff, and other influential people in town. Martin wrote about the many deportments Wells organized, the indictments of Vincent St. John, the search for Barney's bones, and the bomb that went off in Wells's second-floor bedroom that left him with only a few scratches. After a failed attempt to convict St. John for the murder of Arthur Collins when the case went to trial in 1908, Wells was viewed by many as a liar, and he soon lost his influence over Telluride, even though he became the president of First National Bank and of the Western Power Company. As he spent less and less time in Telluride on travels to look after his father-in-law's business interests, he began to have affairs. He lost friends in 1911 when he became embroiled in a bitter lawsuit involving Charles Chase and the Liberty Bell Mining Company. Wells had accused Chase of using Smuggler-Union land for the Liberty Bell. Wells won the case and over $400,000 in damages.

Wells spent the next decade trying to win back friends by wining and dining them with his wife's money until she finally divorced him in 1918, taking her money with her. He left Telluride in 1923 and remarried a beautiful platinum blonde twenty-five years his junior. He continued to have affairs, however, and after a series of failed investments, soon found himself bankrupt. In 1931, in his home in Virginia, he took his revolver from his desk drawer and shot himself in the head.

Ellen covered her mouth and gasped. "I can't believe he killed himself. I didn't think narcissists were capable of that."

"I guess they are when there is nothing left to justify their arrogance," Sue put in. "His money and influence defined him. When that was gone, he felt he had no reason to live."

"How sad," Tanya said. "Even after all the pain he caused others, it's still sad."

"I wonder if he felt any remorse for what he'd done," Ellen added.

"I doubt it," Sue began, "but you never know."

"So, how is his ghost here, if he died in Virginia?" Ellen wondered aloud.

"Evania Glavo's curse," Sue speculated. "Remember? Glavo somehow divided Wells's soul. Maybe one half is here, and the other half is in Virginia."

Ellen sighed. "Let's try to finish the timeline today. I want to sleep in a hotel tonight. Will y'all join me, or do y'all plan to sleep here?"

"As beautiful as this place is," Tanya began, "I wouldn't mind getting one night's sleep. I'm so tired from the restless nights."

"Agreed," Sue said. "I'll go online and book us someplace nice. Maybe I can book the room next to Robin and Ken, in case Ken needs a change of scenery."

Tanya and Ellen shook their heads and laughed.

"Oh, request a late check in," Ellen insisted. "Tonight, we need to ask the ghost of Buck Wells what he did with Glavo's remains. Finding them seems to be our only hope of breaking the curse."

The ladies continued to build out the timeline. The year 1905 contained only two articles—one told of the April 5th appointment of Wells from captain to general of the National Guard to replace Sherman Bell, and the other told of the bombing and killing of Frank Steunenberg, a former governor of Idaho.

Tanya wrote "1906" on the board. "We're nearly done, right? Only two stacks left?"

"Right," Sue confirmed. "And 1906 starts with a bang. According to this February 8th article in the *Telluride Daily Journal*, a man named Harry Orchard confessed to the bombing of Steunenberg and claimed that he was in cahoots with Vincent St. John. Orchard also claimed that Saint paid a man named Steve Adams to kill W.J. Barney and Arthur Collins. Then, on the eighteenth, St. John was arrested and taken to the federal prison in Boise."

Ellen and Tanya gawked.

"That can't be true, can it?" Tanya asked as she made the note on the whiteboard.

"I don't know what to think," Sue said.

"It can't be true because Barney was still alive, remember?" Ellen put in.

"Wait, look at this," Sue began. "It's from the *San Miguel Examiner* and reports that Pinkerton detective McParland took the confession and had taken charge of the case, but the Pinkerton agency had been hired by Wells and the Mine Owners' Association."

"That sounds like a conflict of interest," Tanya pointed out.

"You bet it does," Ellen agreed. "Who was this Harry Orchard, anyway?"

Sue opened her laptop and did a quick search. "Hmm, I found quite a few results on Google. Let me see . . . this article called 'Famous Trials' by Professor Douglas O. Linder says Orchard was a member of the Western Federation of Miners and . . . let's see, it says, and I quote, 'Orchard's career as a paid union terrorist began in 1903 when he blew up the Vindicator mine in Colorado, killing two men, for a fee of $500.'"

"The union had a terrorist on its payroll?" Tanya asked incredulously.

"According to this article, it did," Sue confirmed. "It says, 'Six months later, a bomb planted by Orchard at an Independence, Colorado train depot exploded, killing 13 non-union miners. In his testimony, Orchard also told of other planned killings that for one reason or another did not succeed, all ordered, he claimed, by Haywood and Pettibone—WFM officials. Among the unsuccessful efforts were the assassinations of Governor Peabody and two Supreme Court justices of Colorado and the president of the Bunker Hill Mining Company.'"

"Is there any mention of Vincent St. John?" Ellen asked.

Sue tilted her head to the side. "Let's see. No, it goes on to say, 'Orchard testified that he was hired by Haywood to kill Steunenberg as revenge for the former governor's harsh crackdown on miners in 1899. He assembled an eight-by-four-inch bomb using ten pounds of dynamite and on December 30, 1905, planted it by Steunenberg's side entrance gate.'"

"It doesn't say anything about how or why Orchard implicated St. John in Barney's supposed murder?" Tanya asked.

Sue scratched her chin. "Apparently, it wasn't in his court testimony but in his confession to the Pinkerton detective, McParland. This other source has an excerpt from a book called *Roughneck* written by Peter Carlson that says, 'Before the trial, McParland ordered that Orchard be placed on death row in the Boise penitentiary, with restricted food rations and under constant surveillance. After McParland had prepared his investigation, he met with Orchard over a sumptuous lunch followed by cigars. The detective reportedly told Orchard that he could escape hanging only if he implicated the leaders of the WFM. In addition to using the threat of hanging, McParland promised food, cigars, better treatment, possible freedom, and even a possible financial reward if Orchard cooperated. The detective obtained a 64-page confession from Orchard in which the suspect took responsibility for a string of crimes and at least seventeen murders.'"

"That's extortion," Tanya exclaimed.

"But was any part of the confession true?" Ellen wondered.

Sue shrugged. "It says here that the judge threw out the case against St. John, saying that without a body there can be no trial for the murder of W.J. Barney."

Tanya shook her head. "I'm sure if Wells wasn't already obsessed with finding Barney's bones, he was after that."

"But Barney still wasn't dead," Ellen insisted. Then something occurred to her, hitting her like a ton of bricks. "Oh my gosh, I think I know what happened!"

Sue and Tanya exchanged looks of surprise before turning their eyes on Ellen.

"Well, don't keep us in suspense," Sue insisted.

"Spit it out," Tanya demanded.

Ellen crossed her arms. "I'll tell you what I think, but not until after tonight's investigation. I don't want my theory to compromise our results. I want to speak with Wells without tainting the outcome."

Although Tanya and Sue didn't like being kept in the dark, they didn't object and continued to work on the timeline, noting that 1906 consisted of more indictments and acquittals of St. John for various murders. Other documents also suggested that Wells began to dig up Boomerang Hill in search of Barney's remains. In February of 1907, Steve Adams, who Harry Orchard named as being St. John's gunman in Barney's and Collins's murders, testified about Detective McParland's manipulations, and then later in August, Wells claimed to have found Barney's bones—all but one of the hands, as the limbs had been severed and buried a few feet away from one another. Wells placed the skull in the windows of various store fronts—leaving it for a few days in each store—claiming to have finally found Barney.

But even the presentation of a body did not get Wells the conviction he wanted for St. John.

On November 5, 1907, St. John was shot at three times and was hospitalized for injuries that he survived.

"It can't be coincidental," Ellen insisted. "Wells fails to get a conviction after his seven-years-long search for Barney's body, and the next month there's an assassination attempt on St. John?"

"I agree," Sue said.

On the whiteboard, Tanya wrote, "Did Wells order the hit on St. John?" and circled it. Then she turned to her friends. "I know what Ellen thinks happened."

"Wait a minute," Sue objected. "I'm supposed to be the smart one. Why don't I see what you see?"

"Who says you're the smart one?" Ellen wanted to know.

Tanya put her hands on her hips. "You're the brave one, Sue. I'm the smart one."

"What?" Ellen lifted her chin. "Then what am I?"

"The organized one," Tanya offered.

Ellen shook her head and laughed, knowing that Tanya was just teasing—at least she hoped that was the case. "Let's just get on with this. We're nearly to the end."

Sue lifted a newspaper clipping. "On December 31, 1907, Steve Adams was taken into custody by Wells for the murder of Arthur Collins."

"Wells was relentless," Ellen complained. "I bet he still hoped to somehow tie that murder to St. John."

"Didn't Orchard say that Adams was working for St. John?" Tanya pointed out.

"Yes, but in the case against him, St. John was found innocent," Sue reminded them. "But I think Wells wanted to pin that murder on someone in the union or die trying."

"And, unfortunately, Glavo and Siti weren't union men," Ellen added, "which might explain why Wells didn't go after the real culprits."

Sue held up another clipping. "This article is about the bomb that went off beneath Wells's bed in March of 1908. And there are a few others in the aftermath speculating about who did it. Most people thought the union was retaliating against the indictment of Steve Adams, and a mob apparently went to lynch Adams over it. But Wells is quoted as having said, 'If we get one legal conviction, our troubles with the union will be over. If we make one illegal move, our name is mud.'"

"That's rich coming from a man who used his position as a general in the National Guard for his own purposes," Tanya chided as she made the note.

"This is the last clipping," Sue said. "It's dated July 11, 1908. The *Telluride Daily Journal* reports that Adams is found not guilty."

"I bet Wells wasn't too pleased about that," Ellen muttered.

Sue began typing on her keyboard. "Well, we know how Wells died. Let's see if we can find out how St. John died. Hmm . . . this website says that after his wife died in 1915, he bought a small copper mine, making him ineligible to be in the union."

"That's ironic," Ellen said with raised brows.

"Then, in April 1918 in a trial against all labor unions, all officials received a blanket verdict of ten years," Sue said as she skimmed the website. "He was released on bond a year later during an appeal, but when the appeal failed, he was incarcerated again. Then in 1921, when a friend visited him in prison, she found him in the hole. She wouldn't rest until she got to the bottom of why, after which his record was cleared, and he was released from the hole. He was granted clemency by President Harding in 1923. But, according to this website, Saint caught tuberculosis while in prison and remained an invalid for the rest of his life until he died on June 21, 1929."

"That's so sad," Tanya said before adding the note to the whiteboard. "And so unfair."

"Do you think he's stuck here because he can't let go of how he was treated by Wells?" Ellen speculated.

"That's a good question," Sue admitted. "Why don't we try to find out tonight?"

"Okay," Ellen agreed. "But our priority is finding Glavo's remains."

The warm, inviting glow of the Cosmopolitan Restaurant enveloped Ellen as she stepped through the door, flanked by Sue and Tanya. She hadn't expected a crowd at this hour—late for lunch or early for dinner at four in the afternoon, even on a Saturday. The restaurant's proximity to the gondola station added a sense of liveliness to the area, with people bustling in and out, eager to escape the autumn chill. Ellen was worried about Moseby, whom she'd left in the car in a nest of blankets, because dogs weren't allowed inside the restaurant.

Inside, the air was filled with the rich aroma of seafood, steak, and fresh bread. The restaurant's cozy atmosphere, with its soft lighting and elegant décor, provided a comforting contrast to the tension simmering in Ellen's thoughts. Ellen spotted Robin and Ken at a corner table, already seated. Robin looked nervous, her fingers fidgeting around her glass of water, while Ken's expression was more stoic, though the lines of worry around his eyes betrayed his concern.

Before they reached the table, Sue said in a low voice, "He's just as handsome as I remember him—even when he's not smiling."

Ellen and Tanya chuckled but didn't disagree.

"Sorry we're late," Ellen said as they reached the table. "Traffic was worse than we expected."

"No worries," Robin replied, forcing a smile. "We just got here ourselves."

After exchanging pleasantries and ordering their meals, the group fell into a thoughtful silence. The sound of clinking silverware and murmured conversations from other diners filled the gaps between their words.

"Where are the kids?" Tanya asked after a beat.

"At my mother's," Ken replied. "That's where they hang out during the days."

"The kids are having a blast spending time with their grandparents," Robin added, "while Ken and I take a mini staycation."

"How fun," Sue chimed in. "Especially after what you've lived through over the past four months."

Robin and Ken frowned, the tension returning to their faces.

"This place used to be a union hangout," Ellen said of the restaurant. "The original Cosmopolitan. Buck Wells had it shut down back in 1905."

Ken raised an eyebrow. "Really? I had no idea."

"Seems fitting, given what we're dealing with," Sue added, her tone laced with irony.

Their conversation paused as the server brought over steaming bowls of seafood stew, the rich broth bubbling around generous portions of lobster tail, salmon, sea scallops, and roasted capellini. Ellen inhaled deeply, savoring the fragrant mix of tomato saffron, braised fennel, roasted red pepper, and basil aioli. It was a meal worthy of the effort they'd been putting into the investigation.

As they began to eat, Ellen decided it was time to bring Robin and Ken up to speed. "We've been digging into the history of Buck Wells, Vincent St. John, and Evania Glavo," she said, her voice steady.

"You said Buck Wells is one of two ghosts haunting the house," Robin reminded them. "The Buck Wells in my uncle's painting."

Sue nodded, picking up where Ellen had left off. "Wells was part-owner and manager of the Smuggler-Union Mine, and he wanted to pin the murder of a man named William Barney on union leader Vincent St. John, but the judge wanted a body."

Robin looked puzzled. "Who was William Barney and what happened to him?"

"That's the twist," Sue continued. "William Barney was a stone mason who hadn't been murdered—he'd just left town. He was alive and well, even signed a divorce decree after his supposed death."

Robin and Ken exchanged surprised glances.

"This stew is incredible," Tanya said.

Sue took another bite. "Mm. It really is."

"So, why try to frame St. John for a murder that was never committed?" Ken asked.

"Wells was desperate to take down the union," Ellen explained.

Sue took a sip of her wine. "When he couldn't get St. John for Barney's supposed murder, he tried to tie him to another crime—the assassination of Arthur Collins."

Robin's brows lifted. "The man who was shot in my uncle's house."

"Exactly," Sue confirmed.

"And this is where Evania Glavo comes in," Ellen added after swallowing down a bite of warm, buttery bread. "He was the one who ordered the hit on Collins, but no one knew that until Glavo confessed to Buck Wells four years later."

"So, what did Wells do?" Robin asked, leaning forward.

"Instead of turning Glavo over to the authorities, Wells had him killed," Ellen said quietly, her voice heavy with the weight of history. "Probably because Glavo wasn't a union man."

"And apparently he had Glavo's remains buried in separate locations," Tanya added.

"Can you pass me that butter, Ellen?" Sue asked.

Ellen handed it over.

Ken's brow furrowed in confusion. "Why separate the remains like that?"

"We don't know," Ellen admitted. "But we do know that Glavo cursed Wells so that neither of them would find peace until Glavo's remains are found, reunited, and properly put to rest."

Robin's eyes widened. "And you think our nightmares are part of this curse?"

Sue frowned. "We think Wells is trapped in a loop, reliving his crimes, and whoever sleeps in that house experiences them too—in their dreams."

A tense silence settled over the table as the implications of Sue's words sank in. Robin's voice trembled slightly as she asked, "What about the second ghost?"

Ellen and her friends exchanged knowing glances before Ellen answered, "The second ghost is Vincent St. John, the union official Wells spent a decade trying to convict for the murders of Collins and Barney."

"Why hasn't he moved on?" Ken asked. "Is he cursed, too?"

"We don't know," Sue admitted. "But we're working on it."

Ellen savored the stew while the group sat in tense silence, the young couple processing all they'd been told.

"So, what's next?" Robin asked, her voice tinged with a mixture of fear and determination.

"We need to find Glavo's remains," Tanya said simply.

Ken looked skeptical. "How are you going to do that?"

Ellen set down her spoon, her gaze steady. "We're going to ask Wells where they are—tonight."

The words hung in the air, heavy with the weight of their mission. Ellen could see the doubt in Ken's eyes, the fear in Robin's, but beneath it all was a flicker of hope. They had come this far, unraveling a mystery that had been buried for over a century. Now, they stood on the brink of the unknown, ready to confront the ghosts that haunted the mountain home.

<u>CHAPTER TWELVE</u>

The Search Begins

The sun had barely dipped behind the jagged peaks of the San Juan Mountains, still leaving a few streaks of dusky pink in the twilight sky. The air around Robin's house was crisp, tinged with the bite of early December's cold. Inside the grand home, shadows pooled in the corners as night fell. The three friends—Ellen, Sue, and Tanya—had gathered in the sprawling living room, a space dominated by a massive stone fireplace, an enormous Christmas tree, and high windows that revealed the settling darkness outside.

"We're all set?" Ellen asked, her voice a touch tense over the candlelight between them. She clutched her sketch pad as she glanced at their full-spectrum cameras and other equipment set up around the room.

Sue leaned back in her chair, holding a flashlight. "Let's not waste time. Let's see if we can get them to talk."

Tanya took a deep breath. "I'm ready when you are."

The three women arranged themselves around the dining room table, on which the Ouija board rested, ready for use. But first, Sue insisted on starting with the knocking technique.

She cleared her throat and addressed the darkness with a calm authority, "Spirits of the other realm, we come in peace. We hope to help you to get unstuck, so you can move on to the other side and find peace. We have questions for Buck Wells. Buck, if you're here with us, please knock once for yes."

The room was still, save for the crackle of the fire in the hearth and Moseby's light snoring from the sofa. The seconds stretched on, and just as Ellen began to think nothing would happen, a single, distinct knock echoed from somewhere below them. The three friends exchanged wide-eyed glances.

"Well, that's a start," Sue murmured. She leaned forward, asking, "Are you willing to speak with us?"

Another single knock, clear and distinct.

Ellen's nerves gave way to a steely resolve. "Buck Wells, we know why you're still here. You were cursed by Evania Glavo when he invoked the evil eye, or *malocchio*. You won't rest until his remains are found, rejoined, and properly buried. Do you understand what I'm saying?"

Silence. Then, a single knock.

Sue's eyes narrowed, and she shot Ellen a questioning look before turning back to the unseen spirits. "Buck, were you responsible for Glavo's death?"

One knock.

"Did you kill him?" Sue pressed, her voice edged with urgency.

The atmosphere in the room thickened with tension, as if the very air was holding its breath.

Two knocks.

"If you didn't kill him," Sue continued, "who did?"

Ellen took a deep breath, exhaling slowly as she eyed the Ouija board. "Time to dig deeper," she said quietly, her fingers hovering over the planchette. The others followed her lead, placing their fingertips lightly on the plastic indicator. The temperature seemed to drop as they "opened" the board.

Ellen asked, "Buck Wells, please use this tool to answer our questions. Who killed Evania Glavo?"

The planchette moved slowly, almost reluctantly, spelling out letters: M-C-P-A-R-L-A-N-D.

The three women stared at the board, stunned.

Sue broke the silence first. "McParland? The Pinkerton detective who coerced Orchard's confession? The one employed by Wells?"

Ellen's mind raced. "It makes sense," she muttered. She focused on the planchette again. "Buck Wells, do you know where Glavo's remains are?"

The pointer moved faster this time, more confident in its spelling: A-L-L-B-U-T-O-N-E-H-A-N-D.

Ellen and Tanya exchanged looks of grim understanding.

"All but one hand," Tanya whispered, her face pale in the firelight.

Sue let out a soft gasp. "Oh," she said slowly, as if a light had suddenly flickered on in her mind. "Now I see what you two figured out." Her eyes sparkled with sudden insight. "The bones Wells claimed to be Barney's were also missing a hand. Wells passed off Glavo's remains for Barney's."

"Exactly," Ellen whispered. Then aloud, she asked, "Is that true, Buck Wells? Did you pass off Glavo's remains for Barney's?"

The planchette slid to "YES."

Sue leaned closer to the board. "Buck, where are the remains now?"

U-N-D-E-R-T-H-E-C-E-L-L-A-R.

"Under the cellar," Ellen repeated, her brow furrowing. "You mean under this house?"

Again, the planchette slipped to "YES."

Ellen bit her lower lip. "But where's the missing hand? Buck, can you guess where it might be?"

The board responded: B-O-O-M-E-R-A-N-G-H-I-L-L.

Tanya drew in a sharp breath. "Boomerang Hill," she echoed. "That's where they found the rest of the remains years ago, isn't it?"

Ellen didn't answer immediately. Her mind was racing again, trying to piece together the next steps. "We need confirmation," she finally said, rummaging through her purse and pulling out her dowsing rods. "Let's see where they lead us." Then, with her chin up, she addressed the ghost of Buck Wells. "Please use these rods to show me where you buried Glavo's remains—all but the hand. Move the tips closer together as I move nearer to Glavo's bones. Move the tips apart as I move away from the bones."

As Ellen went downstairs to the game room, her friends followed. The rod tips inched together, letting her know that she was going the right way. As she reached the cellar door, they inched closer still. So far, this method was working. Tanya opened the cellar door and shined her light on the dark steps. Ellen descended with her friends on her heels. The wooden steps creaked beneath them as they descended into the bowels of the house, toward the cellar. The cold down there was sharper, biting into their skin even through layers of clothing.

Ellen held the rods in front of her, their tips swaying slightly as she moved. As they approached the cellar closet, the rods slowly began to pull toward each other. The closer she got, the more the rods tips moved together, until they finally crossed over the exact center of the closet floor.

"Right here," Ellen said, her voice tight with anticipation. "This is where the remains are buried."

Tanya crossed her arms, shaking her head stubbornly. "I'm not digging again," she grumbled. "I always get stuck with the hard work."

"That's not true," Ellen objected, turning to face her friend. "I dig just as much as you do."

The two of them turned to Sue, waiting for her response. Sue, ever the strategist, grinned. "I'll prove to you both that I'm the smart one. We'll call Ken and have him do the digging."

Tanya's eyes brightened, and Ellen couldn't help but chuckle.

"You know, Sue, you really *are* the smart one," Ellen said with a grin.

A half hour later, Ellen headed down to the cellar with her friends on her heels.

"He said he'd be here in fifteen minutes," Sue said.

Tanya smirked, nudging Ellen playfully. "Can't say I'm upset about watching Ken do the dirty work. That man could make a paper bag look good."

Ellen chuckled, though her mind was still occupied with the gravity of their task. "True, but let's not get too distracted by his good looks. We're here for a reason."

"Speak for yourself," Sue quipped, flashing a mischievous grin. "After all the nightmares this house has given us, I think we deserve a little eye candy. Consider it our consolation prize."

They laughed, the sound echoing off the cellar walls, momentarily dispelling the tension that had settled over them since they had arrived. For a moment, Ellen allowed herself to relax, to enjoy the levity her friends brought to the situation. It was a welcome relief from the oppressive atmosphere that had enveloped them since they had begun their investigation.

It wasn't long before they heard footsteps descending the creaky cellar stairs. Ken appeared with a lantern in one hand and a shovel slung over his broad shoulder. Moseby appeared behind him at the top of the steps, wagging his tail as Ken descended. Ken gave them a nod of greeting, his dark hair falling into his eyes as he assessed the task ahead.

"Where do you want me to start?" he asked, his voice calm and steady.

Ellen pointed to the spot in the center of the cellar closet floor, where the ghost had led her with the dowsing rods. "Here should be good. We think that's where the remains are buried."

Ken nodded again and set to work, the muscles in his arms and back rippling and noticeable through his shirt as he drove the shovel into the packed earth. Sue and Tanya exchanged appreciative glances, not even trying to hide their admiration.

"Tell me this isn't the best part of ghost hunting," Sue whispered to Tanya, who giggled in response.

Ellen rolled her eyes, though she couldn't deny that watching Ken work had a certain appeal. Still, as the minutes ticked by and the sound of the shovel scraping against the dirt became the only noise in the cellar, she began to feel increasingly awkward. There was something disconcerting about standing there, watching him toil away while they did nothing.

After ten minutes or so, Ellen cleared her throat, cutting through the silence. "Maybe we should, uh, try to communicate with St. John while Ken digs. See if we can find out why he's still stuck here with Wells."

Sue's teasing grin faded. "Good idea. We've got more to do than just stand around gawking."

Ken, who had overheard, chuckled and shook his head.

Moseby, who had been waiting at the top of the cellar stairs, followed Ellen and her friends up to the main floor, to the dining table, where the Ouija board had been left out. Tanya lit the three pillar candles while Sue sprinkled a bit more salt on the ground at their feet. Ellen turned on one of their full-spectrum cameras before taking a seat at the table with her friends. Once they were settled, Mo went to his spot on the couch by the fire.

Outside, darkness had fallen, but the waning gibbous moon shone brightly on the snowy slopes of the mountains. Ellen took a deep breath and glanced at her friends as they put their fingers beside hers on the planchette and "opened" the board.

"Vincent St. John," Ellen said softly, "we come in peace to help you move on. Are you here with us? If so, please move the planchette to—"

Before she could finish her sentence, the planchette slid to "YES."

Ellen exchanged excited glances with her friends before asking, "Why are you here? Why can't you rest?"

The planchette spelled out P-R-O-T-E-C-T.

Tanya furrowed her brows. "Protect? Protect who?"

They waited in silence as many seconds passed before the plastic indicator began to move again. This time, it spelled out J-O-H-N-S-T-O-N-F-A-M-I-L-Y.

"The Johnston family?" Ellen wondered who that was.

"Robin's uncle was Harold Johnston," Sue reminded them. "That must be Robin's maiden name."

Tanya leaned forward. "Maybe St. John stayed behind to protect the Johnston family from Wells."

The planchette moved to "YES."

"I wonder why," Ellen said. "Is there a connection between St. John and the Johnstons?"

The planchette moved in a circle and returned to "YES."

"What's the connection?" Sue asked.

The planchette spelled out F-A-M-I-L-Y.

"St. John and his wife never had children," Ellen whispered, "but he did have a sister named Helen who had a family. Maybe the Johnstons are her descendants."

The planchette moved to "NO."

"The Johnstons could be descendants of his wife's family," Tanya theorized. "Maybe his wife Clara had a sister or brother that—"

The planchette moved to "YES."

"That's it, then," Sue said with her eyes bright. "We solved the mystery. Wells is here because he was cursed by Glavo, and St. John is here to protect his wife's family's descendants from Wells."

The planchette slid in a circle and returned to "YES."

"Thinking of others even in death," Ellen said thoughtfully. "What a good guy."

Their celebration was cut short when the planchette began to move again. The three friends watched anxiously as it spelled out B-E-W-A-R-E.

Tanya gave Ellen and Sue a worried glance. "Beware of what?"

The planchette spelled out P-O-S-S-E-S-S-I-O-N.

"Is Wells going to possess one of us?" Sue asked.

The planchette slid to "YES."

"Ladies!" Ken's voice carried up from the lower level. "I've found something."

Ellen and her friends jumped to their feet and rushed downstairs. Moseby followed, excitedly wagging his tail.

Using the flashlight on her phone, Ellen led the way down the cellar steps to the closet, where Ken stood, sweaty and waiting.

"Did you find the remains?" she asked as he moved from the doorway to let her and her friends inside.

Moseby, who remained at the top of the stairs, began to growl.

"I told you they'd be here, didn't I?" he said in a teasing tone.

"I believe it was I who told you," Ellen teased back.

With the light from his lantern, Ellen could make out something poking through the four-foot-deep hole he'd dug in the ground.

"It looks like a metal case," Ellen noted. "Can you pull it out of there?"

"It's an ammo box," he said as he wrestled the metal container from the earth. "Hunters use it for storing their ammunition."

"You think Glavo's bones are inside?" Tanya asked from the doorway.

"All but the hand," he replied.

Ellen exchanged a look of bewilderment with her friends. Had they told Ken that bit of information?

"Let's take it upstairs into better light," Sue suggested from the main room of the cellar.

Ken led the way up the cellar steps. Moseby continued to growl.

"Moseby-Mo!" Ellen admonished. "It's okay. Stop that growling!"

Moseby whined and kept his distance as Ken put the container on the coffee table and began to pry it open. The rusty, dark gray metal container was about two feet tall, two feet wide, and one foot thick.

As Ken opened the lid, an acrid smell filled Ellen's nostrils, and she covered her mouth, trying not to be sick.

Tanya pinched her nose and leaned over Ken. "Is that a human skull?"

Ken smirked. "Indeed, it is. Hello, Glavo, my old friend."

The three friends exchanged looks of disapproval.

"I'm usually one for a good joke," Sue began, "but that's not funny, Ken."

"Sorry, ladies."

"And I'd be careful with that," Ellen warned of the skull as Ken was about to reach inside the case for it. "It could easily disintegrate."

Ken closed the lid on the box. "We should go find the hand tonight and get this over with—the sooner the better. I'm sick and tired of the curse, as I'm sure you can imagine."

"It's late," Tanya objected. "Why not go first thing in the morning?"

"It'll be easier to search in the daylight," Ellen added.

"I'm going tonight—with or without you," he declared. "My family has suffered too much already."

"How do you know where to look?" Sue wanted to know.

"We'll summon old McParland on Boomerang Hill, won't we? Isn't that why you're here?"

Tanya furrowed her brow. "How do you know about McParland and Boomerang Hill?"

"You told me, when you asked me to come over this evening," he insisted as he returned to the cellar for his shovel and lantern.

In the few minutes that Ken was downstairs, Ellen turned to her friends. "I don't recall telling him, do you?"

"No," her friends said at once.

"Are we going with him?" Ellen asked them.

"I was wondering the same thing," Sue put in.

"He's forcing our hand," Tanya pointed out. "If we want this done right, we have no choice."

Just then, Ken emerged from the cellar with his shovel and lantern and headed up the stairs to the main level. The three friends and Moseby quickly followed.

CHAPTER THIRTEEN

Boomerang Hill

Ken's voice was low, with the kind of excitement that set Ellen on edge. "If we want to break Glavo's curse, we've got to find his missing hand. And if we want to do that, we need to get to Boomerang Hill tonight."

Ellen stood by the door of Ken's cozy mountain home, rubbing her arms against the cold. Her breath clouded in front of her as she glanced toward the snow-covered trees surrounding the house. She didn't feel ready for another wild goose chase, and she was dead-dog tired.

Sue's voice broke through Ellen's thoughts. "Ken, it's already late. We've been up for hours. You know we haven't been getting good sleep here. Can't this wait until morning?"

Ken, already at the wheel of his hulking, white Infiniti QX80, frowned. "If we wait until morning, state troopers will stop us before we even get close to the lakes. Besides, this thing's built for mountain roads." He patted the dashboard, as though the vehicle were a trusty old steed.

Ellen frowned and glanced down at Moseby, who stood near her feet, growling low in his throat. The tiny dog had been suspicious of

Ken ever since they'd found the remains. Now, Moseby's steady growl made Ellen's gut twist. She bent to pick him up, tucking him into his pooch carrier and slinging it across her chest like a cross-body purse. Keeping him close felt safer somehow.

Tanya shifted from one foot to the other, pulling her jacket tighter. "I don't know," she murmured, her voice wavering. "Ken's probably right about not getting caught, but maybe we should wait. The roads are gonna be icy, and—"

Ken cut her off. "Look, we've got four-wheel drive, brand-new winter tires, and I know these roads like the back of my hand. We'll be fine."

Ellen exchanged a glance with Sue. Neither of them liked the idea, but neither wanted to be left behind, either.

Sue rolled her eyes and threw up her hands. "Fine, but I call dibs on the back seat. I'm not watching you zip around the mountain roads without a guard rail."

Ellen chuckled nervously as they all piled into the SUV, Sue scooting in beside her while Tanya, who was prone to car sickness, took the front passenger's seat. Ellen fastened her seatbelt and adjusted Moseby's carrier, hoping the dog would settle, though his growling didn't let up. She gave his head a soothing pat and tried to ignore the anxious knot forming in her stomach.

Ken revved the engine, giving them all a roguish grin. "Buckle up, ladies."

The vehicle rumbled out of the driveway, snow crunching under the tires as they headed toward the main highway. Ellen watched the trees whip past, their heavy branches frosted with snow and icicles. Ken seemed too comfortable behind the wheel, taking the icy curves at speeds that made her heart race.

"You might want to slow down," Sue piped up from beside Ellen, her fingers gripping the seat. "I mean, not that I'm nervous or anything," she added sarcastically, "but we *are* on a mountain road, and I'd rather not go careening off the edge into oblivion."

Ken laughed, as if her concern was part of the fun. "Don't worry. I've got this. Drove these roads my whole life." His words did little to ease Ellen's worry, especially as they rounded another tight bend with no guardrail in sight. She could feel her palms growing sweaty, clutching the strap of Moseby's carrier for comfort. The little dog gave a huff, as if sharing her tension.

Ellen tried to change the subject, hoping to distract herself from the icy drop just outside her window. "Why's it called Boomerang Hill, anyway?"

Ken glanced at her in the rearview mirror, seemingly unfazed by the precarious drive. "It's named for Boomerang Road, which runs all the way from Telluride to Alta and the Alta Lakes. The thing is, the road doesn't go anywhere else. Once you hit the lakes, there's no other route—so you've got to 'boomerang' back the way you came."

Tanya, leaning forward with white knuckles on the dashboard, muttered, "Sounds like we're the boomerangs tonight."

As they drove farther, the main highway gave way to smaller, rougher roads. Soon they came across a sign that made Ellen's stomach drop: "Alta Lakes Road: Closed for Winter." Ken, as if he hadn't seen it, plowed forward without even slowing.

"Ken!" Ellen gasped. "That road's closed! What are you doing?"

Ken barely glanced at the sign. "Like I said, if we tried this in the daytime, we'd be stopped for sure. But at night, no one's around to bother us."

Sue looked horrified. "And that's supposed to make us feel better? We're driving on a closed road at night, on a mountain, in the ice and snow. How is this a good idea?"

Ken only smiled, focusing on the road ahead. "Trust me. If we don't do this now, we may never get another chance."

The tires crunched over the packed snow, and the road became narrower and more treacherous. The moonlight barely pierced the dense forest. Every bump sent a fresh wave of worry through Ellen, and Tanya had a death grip on the dashboard.

Ellen leaned closer to Sue, whispering, "This is crazy. Why didn't we wait until morning?"

"Because we're idiots?" Sue whispered back, eyes wide as she stared at the road ahead. "I suppose if we die, at least it will be in the company of a beautiful man."

Ellen had no idea how her friend could joke when she was obviously scared out of her mind. She supposed it was a defense mechanism that somehow took over involuntarily.

Tanya turned around in her seat, her face pale. "Maybe we should make him stop. We can turn around."

Before Ellen could agree, Ken's voice cut through the rising panic. "Relax. We're almost there. Just a little farther, and we'll be at Boomerang Hill."

The ladies exchanged glances, none of them comforted by his confidence. Ellen held Moseby tighter as the dog let out a low growl. She stared out the window, wondering if they'd made the wrong choice.

Maybe it wasn't just the ghost of Evania Glavo they had to worry about.

A few minutes later, Ken eased the Infiniti to a stop at the trailhead, the headlights illuminating the start of a narrow, snow-covered path.

"We'll have to walk the rest of the way," he said, putting the SUV in park. He popped the back and climbed out and grabbed a shovel and lantern from the cargo area, his breath visible in the cold air as he spoke. "It's not far—about a quarter of a mile."

Ellen, feeling a shiver of apprehension, gathered Moseby closer, keeping him in his carrier. The little dog was still growling, a low, steady sound that made her more uneasy by the minute. She unbuckled her seatbelt and stepped out into the freezing night.

"I don't know about this," Sue muttered as she followed Ellen out, shining her flashlight on the darkened trail. "It's freezing. What if we don't find anything?"

"Then we're just freezing our butts off for no reason," Tanya replied, pulling her coat tighter. "But we're already here, so let's get this over with."

Ellen glanced at Ken, who was already heading up the trail with the lantern, his shovel slung over his shoulder like some kind of grave robber. She exchanged worried looks with Sue and Tanya but said nothing.

They followed Ken up the snowy incline, their flashlights cutting through the dark. He warned them about the old, rusted cables and ore carts still embedded in the ground, remnants of a once-thriving mining operation. The beams of their lights caught glimpses of twisted metal, half-buried wheels, and scraps of wood sticking up through the snow like skeletal fingers.

"That there," Ken said, pointing to a looming structure in the distance, "was the old sawmill."

The sawmill was tall, its wooden frame half-collapsed, and the remaining structure filled with eerie shadows in the moonlight. Ellen squinted as they passed, certain she saw a figure standing in one of the upper windows. It was gone in the blink of an eye, and she hesitated to say anything, not wanting to seem paranoid.

They continued up the trail, passing the ruins of a general store, according to Ken, but it was now a collapsed pile of timber buried in snow. "And that was the outhouse," he added, nodding toward a sagging structure to their left.

Ellen barely paid attention, her mind racing with questions. She clutched Moseby tightly, her little dog's constant growling and shaking making her increasingly nervous. Something wasn't right about Ken. The way he talked, the way he moved. And his odd familiarity with the cursed history of Evania Glavo didn't help matters.

They reached a sign at the next trailhead: Boomerang Trail. Ken led them further up the hill until they came to a large, nearly intact structure. The wooden building stood out from the rest, almost defying time and decay.

"That," Ken said, "was the mine office and the manager's residence. And up at the top of the hill, behind the boarding house, was where we found Glavo's skull."

Ellen's heart skipped a beat. She stopped dead in her tracks, exchanging looks with her friends. "*We?*" she asked, her voice sharper than she intended. "What do you mean 'we'?"

Ken grinned, his teeth flashing in the cold night. "The people of Telluride, history, whatever." He swung the lantern forward. "Why don't you ladies go ahead and summon McParland? Get him to show us where the hand is buried."

The wind whipped around them, but it wasn't the cold making Ellen shiver. The more Ken spoke, the more she feared something had taken over him—Buck Wells, maybe. Or something worse. She didn't trust him, not anymore.

"I—I think he's possessed," she whispered to Sue.

"Yeah, no kidding," Sue muttered back, her eyes wide.

Ellen swallowed her fear and joined hands with her friends. "Sue, what was McParland's first name?"

Sue frowned, reaching for her phone. "I don't remember. Let me look it up—"

"It was James," Ken said, his voice nonchalant. "James McParland. I know my history."

Ellen felt a fresh surge of dread. How would Ken know that? She hadn't even known that.

"James McParland," Ellen said, her voice trembling slightly. "If you can hear us, we're asking you to come to us. Look for the light of our lantern and flashlights. Follow the sound of my voice. We need your help. Please give us a sign that you're willing."

They stood in silence for a long minute, the cold seeping into Ellen's bones. Just as she started to doubt, Tanya's flashlight flickered.

"McParland? Is that you?" Sue asked, her voice shaky.

The flashlight flickered again. Ellen held her breath, watching as the light dimmed, then brightened. A faint buzzing sound filled the air, coming from the trees behind them.

Ellen quickly pulled out her dowsing rods from her purse. "James McParland," she said softly, "if you're here, please help us. Lead me to where Glavo's hand is buried. Bring the rod tips together when I'm going toward it and move them apart when I'm going away from it."

Holding her breath, Ellen began to walk slowly, the rods twitching in her hands. She felt them pulling her off the trail, past two ruined buildings that looked like they had once been homes. The rod tips moved together, slowly but surely.

"Here," Ellen said, stopping near a patch of snow-covered ground. "The hand is buried here."

Ken didn't waste a second. He struck the ground with the tip of his shovel and began to dig, the sound of the shovel slicing through the frozen earth echoing through the night. The women stood a short distance away in a tight circle, watching as Ken worked furiously.

"He's not right," Tanya whispered, her eyes glued to Ken.

"We need to protect ourselves," Ellen said, her breath coming in cold drags.

"Let's pray together," Sue suggested. "How about the Lord's Prayer?"

The three women bowed their heads and began to recite the familiar words, their voices rising in the darkness. "Our Father, who art in heaven, hallowed be thy name . . ."

As they prayed, Ellen felt a warmth spread through her chest, as though the words were pushing back the darkness around them. Even Moseby, nestled against her, had stopped growling.

Ken, however, seemed more driven than ever, digging with almost manic intensity. He gasped in pain at one point but refused to stop. "I have to end this curse," he muttered, his voice strained. "It has to be tonight."

They stood in silence as he dug, the minutes stretching on endlessly. Finally, after nearly an hour had passed, Ken called out, his voice triumphant. "I've found something. I think it's a finger bone."

Ellen and her friends hurried over, kneeling in the dirt and snow to sift through the soil with their bare hands.

"Be careful," Ellen warned. "If we leave even one bone behind, the curse won't be lifted."

"How many bones does a hand have?" Tanya asked.

Sue pulled out her phone, tapping quickly. "Oh, my gawd, there are twenty-seven. This is going to take all night."

Ellen sighed, brushing dirt off her pants. "Maybe we'll get lucky." She said a little prayer asking God to please help them find the bones fast.

Two hours later, the foursome had twelve bones collected in Ellen's Ziploc bag—less than half of the twenty-seven from Glavo's hand. Her fingers were frozen and painful to the touch, and she was so exhausted that she could barely keep her eyes open.

On the ground beside her, Sue said, "I can't do this anymore, Ken. My entire body hurts."

"Mine, too." Tanya stood up and stretched her legs. "Can we please call it a night and come back in the morning?"

"I second that idea," Ellen said, though Ken didn't stop sifting through the dirt long enough to make eye contact. "Ken?"

"You ladies go wait in the car. I'm not leaving without all twenty-seven hand bones." Ken handed the car key to Tanya.

"Will you help me up?" Sue asked Tanya, extending her hand to her.

After Tanya had helped Sue up, Ellen asked for help, too, and then the three of them, along with Moseby, walked the quarter-mile trek back to Ken's Infiniti.

They were so tired that they walked in silence, and once they were in the car, Ellen curled up with Moseby and said, "I'm going to sleep."

"Me, too," Tanya said. "But it's freezing in here."

"Start the engine and get the heater going," Sue suggested.

Tanya started the engine and, after a beat, said, "Oh, that's better."

"Thank goodness Ken didn't insist that we keep digging," Ellen said, relishing the heat as it moved through the vehicle. "I could barely keep my eyes open."

"And I'm so sore," Tanya moaned.

Ellen looked at the time on her phone. "I can't believe it's almost midnight. I guess it's too late to cancel our hotel reservation."

Sue sighed heavily. "When I fantasized about spending a night with Ken, this was not what I had in mind."

Ellen chuckled and closed her eyes. "Good night."

"Good night," Sue and Tanya replied sleepily.

Ellen's eyes fluttered open as Moseby nudged his cold, wet nose against her cheek. Her little black dog whined softly in the small confines of the back seat of Ken's parked Infiniti. She stretched, groaning as her stiff joints protested the cramped sleeping arrangement.

"Alright, alright," she muttered, sitting up. Moseby hopped into her lap, pawing at her impatiently.

The cabin of the SUV was dimly lit by the soft glow of the morning sun. Ellen blinked as she glanced at the dashboard clock. Nearly seven, she realized, surprised that she had slept so late. Ironically, it had been her best night of sleep on the trip, free of the terrifying nightmares that had plagued her and her friends since their arrival. She turned to look out the window, but there was no sign of Ken. The thought sent a jolt of concern through her.

Tanya, bundled in a puffy coat, snored softly in the front passenger's seat. Sue was sprawled beside Ellen in the back, snoring just as loudly, clearly oblivious to the growing light.

Moseby's insistent whine pulled Ellen from her thoughts. "Alright, you win," she sighed, carefully opening the door. As she stepped out into the snow-covered ground, the cold air chilled her skin, and Moseby bolted into the nearby trees, sniffing excitedly.

Ellen rubbed her arms to ward off the chill as she scanned the area. There was still no sign of Ken. He'd been digging all night up on Boomerang Hill, searching for the remaining hand bones of Evania Glavo. But surely, by now, he should have returned.

She slipped back into the SUV, jostling Tanya awake. "Hey, we need to check on Ken."

Tanya blinked, groggy but quickly coming to. "What time is it?"

"Seven. And Ken hasn't come back yet."

"What?" Tanya groaned, rubbing her eyes. "He can't still be digging, can he?"

"I don't know." Ellen turned to Sue, gently shaking her awake. "Sue, come on, we're going to check on Ken."

Sue stirred, blinking blearily. "What? No way, my back and knees are killing me. You two go ahead. I'll guard the car," she mumbled, curling back up in her seat.

Ellen and Tanya exchanged glances.

"Of course you will," Tanya muttered dryly.

Ellen shook her head, grabbing Mo's leash. "Come on, Moseby."

Mo trotted over to her, and after she leashed him, the three of them set off, making the quarter mile hike up Boomerang Hill. The snow crunched underfoot as they ascended, the early morning air sharp with frost. Ellen couldn't shake the growing sense of dread gnawing at her.

When they finally crested the hill of the Alta ghost town, they spotted Ken crouched behind one of the ruins near the open pit, furiously digging at the frozen earth with his bare hands. His fingers were raw, streaked with blood, the nails torn and caked with dirt. His face, pale and gaunt, was framed by dark circles under his eyes, and his body trembled uncontrollably from the cold.

"Ken!" Ellen called, rushing to his side. "Ken, what on earth are you doing?"

He didn't look up. His breath came in ragged gasps as he continued digging, his voice hoarse as he rasped, "I'm close . . . I'm so close. Just one more bone."

"Ken, look at your hands!" Tanya exclaimed, kneeling beside him. She gently touched his arm, but he yanked it away.

"I don't care," Ken snapped. "I'm too close to stop now!"

Moseby began to growl again.

Ellen felt her stomach twist as she watched Ken. His desperation was palpable, but it wasn't just that. His voice, his mannerisms—everything about him seemed . . . wrong. She had been suspicious before, but now the truth became undeniable. Ken wasn't himself.

"You need to stop. You're hurting yourself," Ellen urged, trying to keep her voice calm.

But he shook his head violently, his fingers still clawing at the ground. "I have to find it. I can't stop . . . not yet."

Ellen exchanged a worried glance with Tanya, her heart hammering in her chest. She knelt beside Ken, the snow soaking through her pants as she began sifting through the dirt. Tanya followed suit, working silently, both of them praying they could find the last bone and end this nightmare.

After nearly an hour had passed, Tanya suddenly gasped, pulling a small finger bone from the earth. "Here! This has to be it!"

Ken's head snapped up, his bloodshot eyes locking onto the bone. A wide, unsettling grin spread across his face. Before they could react, Ken lunged forward, scooping Tanya into his arms with surprising strength. He lifted her into the air, spinning her around as he let out a wild, triumphant laugh.

"Ken, what the—" Tanya began, but her words were cut off as he pressed his lips to hers in a fervent, unexpected kiss.

Ellen's jaw dropped, her mind reeling. For a moment, the world seemed to stop as Ken set Tanya back down, his eyes gleaming with relief.

"Let's get back to the car," Ken said, his voice eerily calm now as he added the final bone to the plastic bag containing the others from Glavo's hand. "We've got what we came for."

Still in shock, Ellen and Tanya followed him down the hill, Moseby padding at their heels, his growl incessant and unrelenting. As Ellen stared at the back of Ken, she couldn't shake the feeling that they hadn't just found Glavo's bones—they'd unearthed something much darker.

Ellen stepped out of the car, relieved that Ken was able to get them back to the house in one piece. She'd offered to drive—they all had—but Ken had insisted that he knew the mountains like the back of his hand and was perfectly capable. The chill of the night lingered in the air, and she pulled her coat tighter around herself before helping Moseby from the car. Beside her, Ken climbed from the driver's seat, swaying on his feet. His hands, red and raw, trembled as he closed the door. The sight of his gaunt face, pale and hollow-eyed after a night of digging, sent a shiver down Ellen's spine. She exchanged concerned looks with Tanya and Sue.

"Ken, you should see a doctor," Sue said, her voice unusually soft for someone who typically came armed with wit and sarcasm. "Those hands . . . you're a mess."

Ken waved her off with a tired grunt. "I'm fine. Just need a shower, a change of clothes, and some sleep."

"We'll drive you back to Telluride," Ellen insisted. "You look like you're going to pass out."

"Hotel's too far," he mumbled, brushing past her. "I'll stay here. In my home. You three figure out the next step with Glavo's curse."

Ellen wanted to argue but stopped herself. There was a weariness to him that went deeper than just physical exhaustion. The man had been through something out there on Boomerang Hill. She felt it in her bones.

Sue crossed her arms. "Will you at least give Robin a call and let her know you're alive?"

Ken paused on the threshold, looking back at them with bleary eyes. "Of course," he muttered before disappearing into the house.

As soon as he was out of earshot, Ellen released a heavy sigh as she set Moseby on his feet. "I don't like this."

Tanya leaned against the door, her face thoughtful. "You think it's Wells? Has he attached to Ken?"

Ellen hesitated. "I think it's possible that Wells hasn't just attached to him but has taken possession of him. We might need to perform an exorcism."

"If we lift the curse," Tanya reasoned, "maybe Wells will move on. The man's been bound by guilt and vengeance for far too long and seems anxious for peace."

"I agree," Sue chimed in. "Priority one is breaking that curse, but it's probably best if Ken stays here away from his family for now."

Ellen nodded, but her mind still churned with possibilities. "Before we can do anything, we need to be absolutely sure that the remains we found belong to Glavo—and that the hand belongs to the rest of the body. If we're wrong, we could make everything worse."

Tanya raised an eyebrow. "And how do you propose we do that?"

Ellen smiled. "I think it's time to call Bob Brooks."

Sue nodded. "My thoughts exactly."

"Come on, Moseby-Mo," Ellen called to her dog. "Let's go inside."

Ellen pulled out her phone and scrolled through her contacts, finding Bob Brooks's number. She put the phone on speaker as she and her friends surrounded the kitchen bar, taking off their coats and scarves, and after a couple of rings, his familiar, deep voice crackled through the speaker.

"Ellen! It's been too long. What can I do for you?"

Ellen quickly filled him in on the situation, the curse, the bones, and Ken's all-night digging expedition. Bob whistled low when she was finished.

"Sounds like you've got quite the case on your hands," Bob said. "I'd love to come out there and help in person, but I'm in the middle of final exams—can't leave my students high and dry. But I think I know someone who can help."

"Who?" Ellen asked, hopeful.

"A forensic geneticist friend of mine, Dr. Elvira McCombs. She's based in Denver. If you're willing to make the drive, I'm sure she'd be interested in the case."

Sue groaned. "That's a six-hour drive from here."

"And the roads will be iced over," Tanya added.

"I wish I knew someone in Telluride," Bob said apologetically.

Ellen smiled. "Thanks, Bob. We'd be willing to make the trip if she can help us identify the bones. We need to be sure."

"I'll call her now," Bob said. "I'll give her your number and let her know how urgent it is. If she's free, I'm sure she'll reach out soon. If she's not, I'll call you back and let you know."

"Appreciate it," Ellen said. "You're a lifesaver."

"Just doing what I can. Good luck out there."

The call ended, and Ellen slipped her phone back into her purse.

"If we do drive to Denver," Sue began, "we should plan to stay the night. It's too far for a day trip." Then, she added, "Hey, maybe we can catch a Broncos game while we're there. Tom would be so jealous."

Tanya laughed softly. "Sure. Let's save some souls first, shall we?"

Ellen exhaled slowly. "I'm starving. Why don't we wait for Elvira's call over breakfast?"

"Sounds good," Tanya agreed, "but I need to clean up first." She wiggled her fingers, still caked with dirt from digging.

Sue grinned mischievously. "You think Ken will mind sharing the shower with me?"

"Yes," Ellen began, "but Wells won't."

Sue shuddered. "Buzzkill. Now, I'm afraid to go down there by myself. Tanya? Come with?"

While Tanya went with Sue to the master bedroom to get clean clothes for Sue, Ellen fed Moseby and then went upstairs to get ready for the day. She chuckled as she climbed into the shower. One thing was certain: She could never be accused of living a boring life.

CHAPTER FOURTEEN

Identifying the Bones

Ellen kissed Moseby on the top of his head as she returned him to his cloth pooch carrier after a quick bathroom break. The chilly December wind whipped through the parking lot of the University of Denver, where Sue had parked their rental in the late afternoon on Monday. She exchanged a glance with Tanya, who was prone to car sickness and wore a look of relief now that the ride was over. It was nearly five o'clock, and the three women were moments away from a meeting they hoped would bring them one step closer to lifting the curse plaguing Robin and Ken and their young family.

"This place looks dead," Sue muttered, her breath visible in the frigid air. "Let's hope this Dr. McCombs isn't like one of those professors who vanishes at 4:59."

"She won't be," Ellen said, more to convince herself than the others. "Bob Brooks wouldn't have sent us her way if she wasn't reliable."

As they approached the building where the criminal justice department was located, Tanya spoke up, her voice tinged with unease, "Do you think she's going to believe us? About the curse, I mean."

Ellen stopped at the door and looked at her friends. "It's not about whether she believes us. We're here for science. Let her figure out what's in those bones, and we'll handle the rest."

The automatic doors slid open with a quiet whoosh, and they were immediately greeted by the warm blast of air from inside the building. After a brief walk down quiet hallways and an elevator ride, they found Dr. Elvira McCombs's office—room 317. Ellen knocked firmly.

"Come in!" called a voice from the other side.

The three women stepped into the cramped, chaotic office. Bookshelves overflowed with journals and textbooks, and the walls were cluttered with framed degrees and photos of McCombs with what appeared to be colleagues at various conferences. In the middle of it all sat Dr. Elvira McCombs—a thin brunette in her late forties, her hair tied back into a loose ponytail. She looked up from her desk and smiled warmly.

"You must be Bob's friends," she said, standing to greet them. "Come on in, and please, have a seat wherever you can find one." Then, she added, "Cute dog."

"This is Moseby," Ellen introduced.

Ellen noticed there were only two chairs, so she motioned for Sue to take one while Tanya pulled up another. Ellen opted to remain standing, too anxious to sit.

Dr. McCombs gestured to the mess around her. "Sorry about the chaos—end of the semester and all that. I'm Elvira. Bob was one of my professors years ago, and when he told me what you all were dealing with, I was intrigued. I'm happy to help."

"We're so grateful that you could meet with us on such short notice," Ellen said, taking a deep breath as she prepared to explain their unusual situation. "We need to identify two sets of remains. We're hoping they belong to the same person, someone who died over a century ago."

Elvira raised an eyebrow, curiosity piqued. "Tell me more."

Sue jumped in, her hands gesturing animatedly as she explained, "The thing is, we're not just trying to identify the remains. There's a curse—a real curse—that's been haunting this young family in Telluride. The remains were buried separately, and we think reuniting them and giving the person a proper burial might break the curse."

Elvira leaned back in her chair, folding her arms. "You can't work with human remains and not have experienced the unexplainable," she said thoughtfully. "I'm not necessarily a believer in the supernatural, but I've seen enough odd things to keep an open mind. I'll do what I can to help you, but science is my realm. Let's see what the bones have to say."

Ellen gave a small nod of relief. "That's all we're asking."

Dr. McCombs stood and gestured to the desk. "So, what do you have for me?"

Ellen reached into her bag and carefully pulled out the two containers: a rusted old ammo box containing the bulk of the old bones and a Ziploc plastic bag containing the hand bones. She placed them on Elvira's desk, the weight of the situation feeling heavier now that they were in the hands of someone who could truly help.

Elvira opened the ammo box first, studying the skull and larger bones inside with a practiced eye. "This looks like it's been through a lot, but I see a few molars still lodged in the skull. I can extract samples from those—they usually provide the best DNA." She then looked at the Ziploc bag, her brow furrowing. "These hand bones are much more delicate. I'll do my best, but I'm worried about whether they'll yield enough material for a proper DNA sample."

"We figured as much," Ellen said. "But we're hoping you can determine if these two sets of bones belong to the same person."

Dr. McCombs nodded. "That's the plan. I'll start by cleaning the samples, which will take several hours. Once that's done, I'll extract DNA from both sets—probably from the teeth, like I said, and then see what I can get from the hand bones."

Sue, always the practical one, leaned forward. "How long does this whole process take? Are we talking several days?"

"Normally, yes," Elvira replied, smiling. "But our department recently acquired a new machine that can generate DNA profiles in about two hours once I've prepared the material. That's after the cleaning and extraction, of course. So, I should have the profiles ready sometime tomorrow afternoon if I get started tonight."

Tanya looked impressed. "That's amazing. Thank you so much!"

Elvira laughed. "Technology keeps us on our toes. Once I have the DNA profiles from both sets, I'll be able to compare them and see if they match. But I'll need more than just comparing profiles if we want to confirm the identity of the remains."

Sue raised an eyebrow. "What do you mean?"

"I can run the profiles through all the major databases—including Ancestry, 23andMe, that sort of thing," McCombs explained. "Of course, if the owner of these remains died long before any of these databases existed, the best I can do is find relatives and make an educated guess."

Ellen's heart lifted slightly. It wasn't a definitive answer, but it was progress.

"I'll work tonight to get the samples prepared," Elvira added. "You should hear back from me by tomorrow afternoon. But there's one thing I'd like in return."

"Name it," Ellen said.

Elvira grinned. "I'd like your permission to publish a paper on this. It's not every day I get to work on such an unusual case, and it could be great for the field."

Ellen exchanged glances with Sue and Tanya. It was a small price to pay for what they needed. "We'd be happy to. Whatever you need."

McCombs slid a waiver across her desk, which they signed without hesitation.

Then Elvira asked, "Would you ladies also be willing to make a donation to our department? It's not a requirement for my help, but I thought I'd put it out there, just in case you were feeling generous. We're always in need of funding to keep up with the latest modern technology."

"Oh, absolutely," Ellen said, glancing at her friends, who also nodded.

After thanking the doctor profusely, the three women and one dog bundled back up and left the office.

As they stepped into the cold afternoon air, Sue rubbed her hands together. "Now, how about we find a good restaurant? We've earned it."

Ellen couldn't agree more, but as they walked toward the car, her mind was already on the bones they had just left behind—and the answers that tomorrow might bring.

Ellen settled Moseby into a nest of blankets in the back seat of their rental car, whispering soft reassurances to the small black dog. His dark eyes blinked up at her sleepily, and with a final pat, she closed the door and turned toward her friends.

"He'll be fine for a couple of hours," she said, more to reassure herself than anyone else. Moseby had become her little shadow. Leaving him behind, even for a nice dinner, made her uneasy.

"Are you sure he's comfortable?" Tanya asked, glancing back toward the car. "I feel bad leaving him there."

Ellen nodded, giving Tanya a small smile. "He's fine. It's not too cold, and he's bundled up."

Sue, already halfway to the entrance of the restaurant, waved them over. "Come on, you two. This place has great reviews, and I'm starving!"

Ellen followed her friends toward Fruition, a chic restaurant nestled in downtown Denver. It was decorated for the holidays, with twinkling lights woven through garlands that adorned the windows and the elegant awning. The air smelled faintly of pine and cinnamon, a festive touch to the otherwise refined atmosphere.

Inside, the ambience was even more impressive. Sleek, wooden tables were organized in rows beneath chandeliers dripping with crystals. A grand fireplace crackled at one end of the room, its mantel decorated with tasteful holiday garlands and flickering candles. The soft hum of conversation filled the air as waiters in black uniforms moved gracefully between the tables.

The hostess greeted them warmly and led them to a cozy corner table near the window. Ellen glanced out at the city street, the cold Denver night softened by the glow of holiday lights strung along the trees.

"I can't believe we found this place," Sue said as she settled into her chair. "I'm telling you, my restaurant radar never fails."

"You do have a knack for finding good spots," Ellen agreed, scanning the menu. Everything looked incredible, but the Olive Oil Poached Halibut caught her eye. "I think I'll go with the halibut."

Tanya nodded. "The swordfish schnitzel sounds interesting. I'll give that a try."

"I'm going for the NY strip," Sue announced with a grin. "Gotta have my steak fix."

After they placed their orders with the waiter, Ellen relaxed in her chair, letting the warmth of the restaurant seep into her bones. It had been a long week in Telluride, and the break from the tension felt like a relief. But as they waited for their food to arrive, Sue pulled out her phone, her expression shifting to something more serious.

"We need to call Robin," Sue said, her voice lower than usual. "She texted that she hasn't heard from Ken since early this morning."

Ellen's stomach tightened. Ken's behavior had been unsettling, to say the least, and Robin deserved to know what was going on. She nodded in agreement, and Sue quickly dialed Robin's number, putting the phone on speaker.

Robin answered after a few rings, her voice tinged with anxiety. "Sue? Everything okay?"

Sue wasted no time getting to the point. "Just wanted to let you know that Ken hasn't been himself since we started digging up Glavo's remains. We're worried that Wells might be influencing him."

Robin's breath hitched audibly through the phone. "I haven't seen him since he left to help you dig. He called this morning to say he was tired after being up all night and was going to sleep at the house, but that's all I've heard."

Sue frowned. "Give him some space for now but keep tabs on him. Maybe give him a call tonight. I think he's staying at the house. If Wells is trying to take hold, it could explain a lot."

"You're scaring me," Robin said, her voice shaking slightly. "Are you saying Ken's . . . possessed?"

Ellen exchanged a glance with Tanya, who looked equally unsettled.

Sue hesitated. "I don't know. But we're doing everything we can to help. We're in Denver now, getting the bones identified. If we can lift the curse on Wells, Ken should be fine."

"And if you can't?" Robin asked, her voice edged with desperation. "Or suppose you do lift the curse, but Wells decides he likes my husband's body too much to leave?"

There was a long pause. Sue finally sighed. "We'll cross that bridge when we get there, Robin. I promise we won't let Wells stay permanently. We've dealt with this before."

Before Robin could respond, the waiter arrived with their food, and Sue said she would check in with Robin tonight before ending the call. The enticing aroma of their meals briefly lifted the somber mood at the table. Ellen took a bite of her halibut, savoring the rich, buttery flavor of the peas and Swiss chard. The meal was delicious, but her mind was elsewhere.

Robin's questions lingered, a knot of worry tightening in Ellen's chest. What if they couldn't help Ken? What if Wells had already taken too strong a hold?

As the evening wore on and their plates emptied, Ellen found herself anxious to leave the elegant warmth of the restaurant and get back to Telluride. There was still so much left unresolved, and the stakes seemed higher than ever.

The next morning after a wonderful night's sleep curled up with Moseby in an Embassy Suites in Denver, Ellen found her friends in the kitchenette drinking coffee in their pajamas.

"Good morning," Tanya greeted. "Sleep okay?"

"Yes," Ellen replied. "The best sleep of the trip."

"It's amazing what a night without a supernatural curse can do for a girl, isn't it?" Sue teased.

"Absolutely," Ellen agreed.

"Are you still game for Meow Wolf?" Tanya asked, her blue eyes bright. "It's supposed to be really different from the one in Santa Fe."

"Definitely," Ellen said. "Sue?"

"As long as we stick together this time," she said. "It's such a maze and so distressing when we can't find one another."

"I agree," Ellen admitted. "And I could use the distraction from this waiting game."

"I wonder when Elvira's going to call," Tanya said before taking another sip of her coffee. "What if the bones don't belong to Glavo?"

Sue gave a nervous laugh. "Then we're back to square one."

"Not square one," Ellen corrected, "but yeah, it would definitely be a bummer."

Ellen shifted Moseby in his cloth carrier, adjusting the strap across her torso as she stood outside Dr. Elvira McCombs's office door. The familiar weight of her little dog provided some comfort, but her nerves fluttered in anticipation. They had spent two hours touring Meow Wolf, an immersive art museum and a much-needed distraction from the tension surrounding the bones. But now, back on the University of Denver campus, reality settled in, heavy as the cold winter air.

Her fingers brushed the door, giving a light knock before she could second-guess herself. Moseby poked his head out, his tiny nose twitching as if sensing her anxiety.

Sue and Tanya stood beside her, both unusually quiet. Ellen stole a glance at Tanya, who was bouncing on her heels, her usual energy barely contained. Sue, ever composed, merely folded her arms, her gaze fixed on the door.

After a moment, it swung open, revealing Dr. Elvira McCombs. The forensic geneticist greeted them with a warm smile and stepped aside to let them in.

"Come in, ladies. I have the results you've been waiting for."

Ellen's heart raced as she followed the doctor inside, Moseby's head still poking out, his dark eyes wide. The chaotic office was brightly lit, and a third chair had been brought in to accommodate them. Dr. McCombs motioned toward the chairs in front of her desk, handing each of them a printed copy of a DNA profile.

"What did you find out?" Sue asked eagerly the moment she sat down. "Were you able to identify the bones?"

Elvira took a seat behind her desk, glancing down at the paperwork before her. "Unfortunately, I couldn't get a clean enough sample from the phalanges and hand bones, but I did have success with the molars." She paused, giving them a moment to process. "And I was able to match the profile those samples generated with living relatives across multiple databases."

Ellen felt her breath catch. This was it. This could be their answer. "Any relatives by the name of Glavo?" she asked, her voice tight with hope. Her fingers crossed unconsciously on both hands.

Dr. McCombs smiled slightly, understanding their anticipation. "Yes. But the closest living relative, a grandson, in fact, is a man named Antonio Zadra. And although his son is deceased, he has two living grandsons, Dante and Marco."

The names hung in the air, the revelation dropping like a weight between them. Ellen exchanged wide-eyed looks with Tanya and Sue.

"This is Dante's great-great-grandfather?" Tanya's voice came out barely above a whisper, the shock evident in her expression.

"Oh, do you know Dante Zadra?" Elvira asked with surprise.

"Not well," Ellen explained. "He was our tour guide in Telluride."

Sue frowned, her brow furrowing. "Does that mean these remains don't belong to Evania Glavo?"

Dr. McCombs tilted her head slightly, her analytical gaze softening with patience. "They can only belong to Evania Glavo if Evania was also Dante Zadra's great-great-grandfather."

Ellen blinked, the words taking a moment to sink in. They'd been working under the assumption that these were Evania's bones. The whole case was becoming one giant roadblock—unless Dante had been wrong about the identity of his great-great grandfather.

The room seemed to hold its breath for a moment before Ellen finally broke the silence. "Is there any indication that the hand bones from the plastic bag could have come from the same person as the other remains?"

Dr. McCombs gave a slight nod. "It's possible. The skull and other remains in the metal box were better preserved, but based on the appearance of the bones, I would say their owners died around the same time and were of similar age when they died, but that's as much as I can tell."

Ellen swallowed, still reeling from the shock. "Thank you, Dr. McCombs," she said, her voice steadying as she gathered the remains from the doctor's desk. "We really appreciate your help."

The others followed suit, thanking the doctor as they stood. Once the remains were secured and they'd said their goodbyes, they exited the office and stepped into the cold Denver afternoon, the tension from moments ago still lingering between them.

Ellen sighed, leashing and setting Moseby on the ground. The poor dog had been patient through everything and was happy now for a bit of freedom as they walked across the campus to their rental.

When they reached the Navigator, Tanya climbed into the front passenger's seat beside Sue, who was already gripping the steering wheel, her mind clearly turning over the new information.

"What should we do next?" Tanya asked, pulling the door shut with a quiet thud.

"Let's get our things from the hotel, check out, and head back to Telluride," Sue suggested. "On the way, we'll call Dante and arrange to meet with him. Maybe his Nonno knows something about *his* grandfather that will help us figure out where to go from here."

Ellen slid into the back seat, still clutching the folder with the DNA results. Was it possible that Dante had been mistaken about the identity of his great-great-grandfather? Why else would his ancestor's bones have been buried in the cellar beneath the Smuggler-Union Office and Residence?

As Sue started the car and they pulled away from the campus, Ellen couldn't help but feel a mix of relief and dread. They were closer to the truth, but what exactly that truth would reveal was still a mystery—one that, like the ghosts haunting them, refused to rest.

CHAPTER FIFTEEN

An Exorcism

Ellen leaned her head against the cool window of the black Lincoln Navigator, her gaze unfocused as she stared at the passing Colorado landscape. Snow-covered pines blurred into a wall of white and green, broken up only by the occasional rock formation. Moseby snuggled on her lap, his ears twitching at the sounds of the engine. Sue drove with her usual confidence, her hands relaxed on the wheel, while Tanya sat in the front passenger's seat, her eyes scanning the road ahead.

The tension in the car felt thick, as if they were carrying the weight of their news from Denver all the way back to Telluride. While the DNA results hadn't confirmed that the bones belonged to Evania Glavo, they *had* confirmed that they belonged to Dante's great-great-grandfather. Was it possible that they were one and the same? At any rate, the mystery had deepened, and now they had even more questions than answers.

"All right, let's see if Dante's around," Sue said, keeping her tone light. She pressed a few buttons on the dashboard, connecting a call through the car's speaker system. After a few rings, Dante's gruff voice crackled over the line.

"Dante's Mountain Tours, how can I help ya?"

"Hey, Dante, it's Sue from Ghost Healers, Inc. We've got some interesting news about human remains we believe belong to Evania Glavo." She glanced briefly at Ellen in the rearview mirror. "You might wanna hear this in person."

There was a brief pause before Dante responded, his voice low with interest, "You've got me curious. Come by my office tomorrow morning, say around eight?"

"Perfect. See you then."

As soon as the call disconnected, Sue tapped the console again and dialed Robin's number. Ellen's stomach tightened. This was the call she dreaded.

Robin picked up almost immediately, her voice panicked and brittle. "Sue! Oh, thank God, I've been trying to reach you all. It's Ken—he's been arrested."

Ellen straightened in her seat, feeling the cold tendrils of dread unfurl in her gut. She exchanged a glance with Tanya, whose eyebrows shot up in alarm.

"What happened, Robin?" Sue asked, her voice calm but serious.

Robin's words tumbled out in a frantic rush. "He went down to the Tomboy Tavern last night, and I don't know what got into him. He assaulted two young women, and apparently tried to kiss one of them, then started a fight with the bartender. He's never been like this, Sue. They've thrown him into the county jail. He spent last night there. I don't know what to do. I'm afraid to post bail and have him around me and the kids."

Ellen closed her eyes and rested a hand on Moseby, trying to ground herself. She had known things were bad with Ken, but this?

"You did the right thing," Tanya assured her.

Robin's breath hitched. "I think so, too, but I'm scared. Ken's not . . . Ken anymore."

Sue exhaled softly, leaning back in her seat. "Robin, keep yourself and the kids safe. We'll head straight to the jail and help your husband. I promise you, he's still in there."

"Thank you," Robin's voice wavered, thick with tears. "I don't know what I'd do without you all. I just—he can't come back home like this. Not until we know he's—"

"We understand," Ellen finally spoke, her voice quiet but steady. "Stay at the hotel with the kids. It's safer for you there."

The call ended, leaving a hollow silence in the car. Sue gripped the wheel a little tighter, and Tanya crossed her arms, leaning back into the passenger's seat.

"So," Tanya said after a long pause, "We're doing this tonight?"

"We don't have much choice," Sue replied. "We need to get Ken out of jail before something worse happens."

Ellen's mind whirled as she recalled what Father Yamamoto, a priest they'd met in Santa Fe, had told them about exorcisms. "We'll need rope to tether him. People can get unnaturally strong when they're possessed."

Tanya nodded. "And something to purify the space. Sage, incense, a bell—anything to drive out negative energy."

Sue tapped her fingers on the wheel. "We've got sage and holy water. I'll call Robin back and ask if they've got rope in the garage."

"No," Tanya objected. "That will only frighten her more, Sue. Let's just buy some from a hardware store."

"Maybe you're right," Sue relented.

Moseby stirred in Ellen's lap as she adjusted her grip on him, her fingers brushing through his fur. The little dog was more sensitive to spirits than any of them; he always knew when something was wrong.

"We're going to need more than just some rope," Ellen said softly. "We're going to need a miracle."

Sue and Tanya exchanged grim looks. There was no turning back now. The road ahead promised to be long—and dangerous.

Sue pulled the car into the gravel lot of the San Miguel County Jail, the headlights catching the outline of the old stone building. It looked imposing against the dark backdrop of the mountains, a squat structure with barred windows that had likely seen its fair share of troubled souls. Ellen shifted in her seat and took a breath, casting a glance at her two friends in the front seat. Moseby sat alert beside her, as if sensing the tension in the air.

"Here we go," Ellen muttered as she put Moseby into his cloth carrier and opened her car door.

Sue and Tanya followed suit, each wearing a grim expression.

The cool mountain air brushed against Ellen's face, and an evening chill worked its way down her spine, as Tanya led the way to the building.

Inside, the jail was all institutional gray and beige, the air smelling faintly of bleach. Ellen approached the desk, where a tired-looking deputy sat behind a partition. He glanced up, clearly unimpressed by the three older women standing before him.

"We're here to bail someone out," Ellen said, trying to sound more confident than she felt.

The deputy gave a slow nod and slid a clipboard toward her. "Name?"

"Ken . . . uh," Ellen turned to Sue.

"Kenneth O'Leary," Sue finished for her.

Ellen fumbled for her reading glasses to sign the paperwork. Sue hovered over her shoulder, craning to see the form.

The deputy took the clipboard back and tapped the paper. "Do you have cash to pay the bail? Otherwise, you'll need to post bond during business hours."

"How much is it?" Ellen asked.

"Five hundred," the deputy replied.

Ellen glanced at Sue and Tanya. They nodded in unison, pooling their money.

"We've got cash," Sue said, arranging their hundred-dollar bills into a neat stack before handing them over.

The deputy eyed it, gave a shrug, and counted the money. "It'll be a minute. I'll have someone bring him up from holding."

The three women found seats in the waiting area, where the plastic chairs were as uncomfortable as they were ugly. Moseby sat on Ellen's lap in his carrier, his little head darting around at every sound. He let out a soft growl, and Ellen shushed him, patting his head absently. Tanya drummed her fingers together, while Sue tapped her foot, humming something under her breath.

"This place gives me the creeps," Tanya muttered.

Ellen didn't argue. Something about the jail's cold, unfeeling atmosphere made her skin crawl. But it wasn't just the building. She couldn't shake the feeling that the real problem would arrive with Ken. He wasn't himself. Hadn't been since that night on Boomerang Hill when they'd uncovered what they hoped were Glavo's hand bones. And it was clear to Ellen that the ghost inside Ken didn't want to leave.

Finally, the metallic clink of a door opening echoed down the hall, and Ken appeared, escorted by a stone-faced officer. Ken's eyes were shadowed, his face gaunt, but it was the way he moved that unnerved Ellen. There was a stiffness, a tension in his posture, like a man at war with his own body.

"Ken!" Sue called, rising to greet him with an awkward, cheerful wave. But Ken barely acknowledged her. His eyes, dark and hollow, flicked toward Ellen, Tanya, and then down to Moseby. The dog's growl grew louder, and Ellen had to hold him tight to stop him from lunging from his carrier.

"Come on, Ken. Let's get you home," Ellen said softly, standing to join him.

Ken nodded once, but there was no relief in his expression. He wasn't happy to be out of the jail, and he certainly wasn't eager to return to the house.

The drive back to Ken's mountain home was tense, the narrow road winding through the thick darkness beneath a waning moon obscured by clouds. Ellen glanced at Ken beside her in the back seat, wishing Moseby would stop his incessant growling.

"You aren't helping," she said to the dog. "Stop that, Moseby. No growling."

The dog paid her no mind.

Ken sat beside them, staring out the window, his fingers twitching occasionally as though resisting the urge to lash out at her dog.

"So," Ken said after a long silence, his voice rough. "What did you find out? About the bones?"

Ellen exchanged quick looks with Tanya and Sue. She didn't want to say it, but there was no point in lying to him. "We ran into a bit of a hitch. The bones . . . they're not officially identified yet. We've got an appointment in the morning to, hopefully, clear things up."

Ken's reaction was immediate. His hand shot out, slamming against the window with such force that the entire car jolted. Ellen gasped, her heart hammering. For a terrifying moment, she thought the glass had cracked, but when she stole a glance, there was no visible damage.

"Dammit!" Ken growled, his eyes flashing with something far too dark, far too wild to be entirely his own. Ellen knew in that instant it wasn't Ken she was seeing—it was Buck Wells.

Sue glanced back from behind the wheel, trying to calm him down. "Hey, hey, Ken. We're on it. We'll have answers soon. We just need to confirm they're Glavo's bones, that's all."

Ken's lip curled in a snarl. "They're his, alright. I should know. I'm the one who put them there."

The car fell into a shocked silence. Ellen felt a chill race down her spine. Even Moseby seemed to freeze, his tiny body pressed against hers for comfort. Ken's eyes, cold and accusing, seemed to bore into hers. She looked away, unable to hold his stare.

"Ken," Tanya said cautiously, her voice steady. "We'll figure this out. We just need a little more time."

Ken didn't respond. He turned his gaze back to the dark forest outside, his jaw clenched tight. Ellen knew they were running out of time. The ghost inside Ken wasn't going to wait much longer.

Finally, they reached the house, the lights from the Christmas tree flickering through the enormous windows like a beacon in the night. But tonight, their beauty felt overshadowed by the oppressive energy Ken carried with him.

Sue parked the car, and Ken stepped out, his movements slow and deliberate, like someone wading through deep water. His eyes flickered toward the house, and, just for a moment, Ellen thought she heard him growl.

Ellen quickly leashed Moseby and gave him a chance to do his business while the others made their way to the door.

Ken pushed the heavy, wooden door open, and they entered. Ellen and Moseby, who hadn't stopped his incessant growling except to pee, followed behind. Her nerves prickled with every step. They had to tread carefully. Ken—or rather, the ghost of Buck Wells—was still fully in control, and they needed him to let his guard down.

"Ken," Sue said lightly, her voice steady. "Why don't you go lie down? It's been a long day."

Ken shook his head, a sly grin tugging at his lips. "I'm not that tired. But maybe a glass of wine would help." He strolled toward the hearth, crouching down to inspect the embers. "I'll get a fire going."

Ellen shared a quick look with Tanya. This was going to be harder than they'd thought. Tanya patted her purse and signaled with her head to follow her to the kitchen.

To Ken, Ellen said, "Great idea. We'll grab that wine while you tend to the fire."

In the kitchen, the three women moved quickly, speaking in hushed tones.

"Remember the Lorazepam my doctor gave me for flying? I've only used it once," Tanya said as she opened the bottle and poured out three pills. "Crush them into his glass of wine. We need to get him to fall asleep."

Sue grabbed a corkscrew, and Ellen found a large glass, trying not to let her hands shake. Moseby, sensing the tension, growled at the sound of Ken moving about in the next room. Ellen rubbed his head soothingly, but nothing seemed to console him.

"I'll take Mo upstairs. He's going to get us all caught if he keeps growling at Ken," Ellen muttered, scooping Moseby up and hurrying to the stairs. She ran to her bedroom, gently placing Moseby on her bed.

"Stay here, boy," she whispered, closing the door behind her and hurrying back downstairs.

When Ellen returned, a roaring fire crackled in the hearth, but it did nothing to quell the chill in the air caused by the ghost of Buck Wells. Ken was already seated on the couch, staring into the fire, his face lost in the flickering glow. A glass of red wine waited for him on the coffee table.

"You've done a good job with the fire," Sue said, sitting down across from him and pushing the glass closer. "But you should really take it easy tonight. You've been through a lot."

Ken eyed the wine for a moment, then picked it up and took a long drink. Ellen let out a breath of relief. Tanya sat beside her, watching carefully as Ken began talking.

"You know," Ken started, his voice low, almost dreamy, "I met two girls at the Tomboy Tavern last night. Haven't seen such beautiful women in a long time."

Sue's eyebrow arched. "I'm sure Robin would appreciate hearing about that."

Ken let out a sharp laugh, shaking his head. "Ah, Robin. She's beautiful too, but . . . these women, they were something else."

Ellen could see the wine was working. Ken's eyes were half-lidded, and his words were starting to slur. He slumped back into the couch, blinking slowly.

"Maybe you should go to bed," Tanya suggested quickly. "You need your sleep."

Ken groaned and nodded. "Yeah. Maybe you're right. I do feel quite sleepy all of a sudden."

He stood but swayed dangerously, nearly tipping over before Ellen and Tanya rushed to his side, each taking an arm to steady him. Together, they guided him downstairs to the master bedroom, where Sue quickly removed his shoes.

"Rest up, Ken," Sue said softly, but there was an undercurrent of urgency.

Once they were sure he was deeply asleep, Tanya dashed upstairs to retrieve the rope they'd brought, and the three women worked together to tie Ken's wrists to the headboard, making sure the knots were secure.

"He's out cold," Ellen whispered, watching Ken's chest rise and fall in heavy breaths. But even in sleep, he seemed restless, twitching occasionally as if fighting an unseen force.

"He sure is a beautiful man," Sue said admiringly. "It's too bad we couldn't have tied him up under different circumstances."

Ellen belted out a laugh but quickly covered her mouth, worried she'd awaken Ken.

Tanya pulled out a bundle of sage, lighting it and waving the smoke over Ken's body, while Ellen uncorked a vial of holy water.

They began the exorcism, standing at each side of the bed. Ellen's voice was strong and commanding as she spoke, "Buck Wells, we know you're in there. You don't belong in this body. It's time to return to where you came from."

Ellen dipped her fingers in the holy water and flicked it onto Ken's brow. "Buck, leave Ken's body. Go back to the cellar where you were bound. We'll help you find peace by lifting Glavo's curse, but only if you let Ken go."

Ken's body jerked violently, his face contorting in a silent scream. His eyes shot open, but they weren't Ken's—they were dark, cruel, filled with fury.

"You can't stop me," he growled, his voice deep and otherworldly. "You don't know what I'm capable of."

Sue cried out in a strong, commanding voice, "We call upon the power of God to help us rid Ken's body of this unholy spirit. Father, we entreat you to save this man, Ken O'Leary, from the evil fiend possessing him."

Ken's body convulsed, the struggle intensifying.

Ellen flicked more holy water onto Ken's face, and he hissed and writhed with pain.

"End Ken's agony, heavenly Father, and banish the ghost of Buck Wells to the cellar below us," Sue continued with determination.

"Please, God!" Tanya cried as she pressed her hands together in prayer. "We beg of you!"

The three friends continued their prayers and admonitions for at least another hour before they noticed a change in Ken. Slowly, the tension in his muscles eased. His eyes fluttered shut, and the room fell eerily quiet. The air seemed to lift, and Ken lay still, breathing softly.

Ellen worried it was an act—that the ghost was still in there. "Ken?" she asked. "Are you with us?"

When his eyes opened again, he asked, "What? I can't keep my eyes open."

Ellen, trembling with relief, removed her *gris-gris* bag and tied it around his neck. "Wear this, for protection. You've been through a lot."

Sue untied one of his wrists while Tanya untied the other.

Then, Sue gave him her tourmaline ring. "For extra protection. Don't take it off."

Tanya smiled gently. "Try to go to sleep, now. We'll call Robin and let her know that you're home safe."

Ken nodded weakly, too dazed from the effects of the Lorazepam to protest.

"Oh, I almost forgot," Sue said, taking a few steps back toward the bed. "Hey, Ken? Ken?"

Still suspicious, Ellen moved beside Sue. "Hey, Buck?"

Ken's eyes fluttered open. "Yeah?"

Ellen and her friends exchanged looks of alarm.

Ellen quickly said, "Get some rest, okay?"

"Okay," he replied, closing his eyes.

Once they were upstairs on the main floor, Sue said, "I guess that did a fat lot of good."

Ellen whispered, "We need to add more protections to ourselves tonight, too, just in case you-know-who attempts to possess one of us."

"Agreed," Sue said. "And I guess I'm sleeping upstairs tonight."

Tanya lifted her brows. "Not unless you want to share with Ken."

"Under any other circumstances, I might be tempted," Sue teased.

"But that's not Ken," Ellen said solemnly.

"No, but maybe lifting the curse will get him to move on," Tanya reminded them. "Let's try to get some sleep. We've got to be up early for our meeting with Dante."

"Can I sleep with you in Dex's room?" Sue asked Tanya as they headed up the stairs. "I have some ear plugs you can use to block out my snoring."

"As long as you don't make any moves on me," Tanya teased.

"I can't make any promises," Sue said with a laugh.

Ellen followed her friends up the stairs, knowing that they used humor to deal with trauma. It was the only way they could bear things sometimes. "I hope the nightmares don't return tonight."

Sue glanced back at her. "Let's pray the Lorazepam keeps Buck out of commission."

After Ellen said goodnight to her friends and rejoined Moseby in her room, she wondered if they'd made a mistake in leaving Ken untied.

CHAPTER SIXTEEN

The Evil Eye

Ellen stirred in bed as the first light of dawn crept through her window Wednesday morning, painting the walls with a soft, golden hue. She stretched, her joints creaking slightly as Moseby perked up beside her, his eyes already bright with anticipation for the day ahead.

"Alright, Moseby, let's get to it," she said with a smile, patting the dog's head. He responded with a wag of his tail.

After a quick shower, Ellen dressed in a warm sweater and brown trousers, brushing through her ash-blonde hair. As she finished, she glanced outside the window. The world beyond was breathtaking—the snow that had blanketed the landscape for days was now slowly melting, revealing earth and stone beneath. The towering mountains, dusted with snow, stood majestic under the clear, blue sky.

"Come on, Moseby," Ellen said as she clipped his leash on. They headed downstairs together, expecting to see Sue and Tanya already up and about. But the house was eerily quiet. The usual morning clatter of Tanya making coffee or Sue talking about the posts on her Facebook feed was absent. Odd.

Ellen shrugged, heading to the front door. "Let's get you outside for a bit," she murmured to Moseby, opening the door and stepping onto the circular drive where the snow had melted into white slush. The crisp air greeted them, fresh and invigorating, and the once-muted landscape buzzed with life. Birds flitted through the fir trees, their songs echoing in the stillness. The distant sound of a stream, swollen with melting snow, added to the peaceful atmosphere.

Moseby busied himself sniffing around and taking care of his morning routine while Ellen breathed in the mountain air, appreciating the serenity of the moment. The quiet was a welcome reprieve from the recent chaos.

Once Moseby was done, they headed back inside. Ellen poured a bowl of food for him and started a pot of coffee, the comforting smell filling the kitchen. She glanced at the clock. It was getting late, and there was still no sign of Sue or Tanya. She hustled up the stairs to wake them.

Ellen knocked on the door to Tanya's room, "Rise and shine, you two!" she called out, before opening the door. Both women were still asleep, each clinging to the opposite side of the bed.

Without moving, Sue answered, "Alright, alright, I'm up."

Tanya sat up, stretched her arms, and gazed out the window. "Looks like a beautiful day. Did either of you have any nightmares?"

"I don't remember them if I did," Ellen replied.

Sue yawned. "Same here. No nightmares. Guess the drugs kept Wells at bay." She sat up and added, "Tanya's snoring . . . now that's another story."

"Maybe *you* should have worn the ear plugs," Tanya said.

"I did," Sue said as she popped them out. "Not that they did much good."

"Sorry," Tanya said.

"I snore, too," Sue reminded her. "I know it can't be helped. It is what it is." She turned to Ellen. "Is Ken up?"

"I haven't seen him yet," Ellen replied.

Sue slipped on her robe and house shoes. "I need to get into that room for a clean change of clothes."

"I'll see if he's up," Ellen offered.

She made her way downstairs to the master bedroom, Moseby following behind. The door was slightly ajar, and when she pushed it open, her heart sank. The bed was empty, the blankets in a twisted pile. She quickly glanced into the adjoining bathroom, but it was also empty.

Her pulse quickened as she hurried down to the cellar, hoping against hope that Ken might be there. But no—there was no sign of him.

Ellen raced back upstairs with Mo on her heels. "Ken's missing," she blurted out to Sue and Tanya, who were just pouring cups of coffee.

Tanya's eyes widened. "Are you sure? Could he have just stepped out for a walk?"

"Moseby and I were out earlier and saw no sign of him," Ellen insisted, her voice tight with worry.

"Did he take the rental car?" Sue asked.

Ellen headed to the garage, where their rental car sat untouched. "No," she called back. "And his car was impounded after his arrest. He couldn't have taken it."

The three women exchanged concerned looks.

"Let's call Robin," Tanya suggested.

Sue grabbed her phone and dialed Robin's number. After a few rings, Robin picked up, but she hadn't seen Ken either.

"We need to keep moving," Ellen said, her voice steady despite her mounting concern. "Let's head to Dante's office and figure this out after our meeting."

Sue and Tanya quickly dressed, and then they all piled into the Lincoln Navigator, Ellen sitting in the back seat with Moseby at her side. As they drove down the winding road into town, Sue suddenly hit the brakes.

"There!" she pointed.

Walking along the side of the road, Ken trudged slowly, his eyes distant, his body moving as if in a trance.

"Ken!" Ellen called as Sue rolled down the window. "Get in the car!"

Ken turned to them, a scowl forming on his face. "I'm fine walking. People used to walk these roads all the time."

Ellen exchanged a worried glance with Tanya. "Ken, it's not safe. You could get hit by a car."

Ken shrugged. "I'm not worried. I've been walking these roads longer than you know."

"Come with us to our meeting about the bones," Sue prompted.

At the mention of the bones, Ken's expression changed, and a brightness came into his eyes. Without another word, he opened the door and climbed into the back seat beside Ellen and Moseby. The dog began to growl softly, the hairs on his back rising as he eyed Ken.

"Tanya," Sue began, "why don't you text Robin and let her know we found him?"

"Will do," Tanya replied.

A few minutes later, they arrived at Dante's Mountain Tours. The office was small, and cluttered papers and maps were strewn across an old, wooden desk. After introducing Ken and Dante, Ellen wasted no time.

"The bones were analyzed by a forensic geneticist, Dante," Ellen said, her voice calm but direct. "She's certain they belonged to your great-great-grandfather."

Dante's eyes widened. Before he could respond, Sue asked, "Is there any chance your great-great-grandfather was Evania Glavo?"

"What? Why would you ask me that?" he asked, his face twisted with bewilderment.

"It's the only thing that makes sense," Ellen explained. "We found his remains buried in the cellar beneath the old Smuggler-Union Office and Residence, where we believe Glavo was buried."

Dante's hand trembled slightly as he reached for his phone. "There's only one person who could know," he muttered, dialing quickly. His face was tight with anxiety as he placed the phone on speaker. The room fell into a thick, expectant silence, the quiet broken only by Moseby's soft breathing.

After a few rings, a frail voice answered from the other end. "Dante, what's going on?"

"Nonno," Dante began, his voice wavering, "I need to ask you something important. It's about our family—about your grandfather. Was he really Ezra Zadra . . . or was he Evania Glavo?"

A pause hung in the air, stretching long enough to make Ellen's stomach twist. She glanced at Ken, whose face remained impassive, though a storm was clearly brewing behind his eyes.

"Why are you asking me this now?" Dante's grandfather finally responded, his voice sharp with surprise.

"We've found his remains, Nonno," Dante said, his voice strained. "Some paranormal investigators—they found his bones, but they're saying they belonged to Evania, not Ezra. Is that true? Did we have it wrong?"

The silence from the other end of the phone was deafening. Everyone in the room held their breath, waiting. Finally, Dante's grandfather spoke again, his voice softer, more reflective.

"They found him? After all these years? *Dio mio* . . . Dante, listen to me. Evania was my biological grandfather, yes. But he went missing when he was very young, not long after my father was born. My father was raised by Evania's cousin, Ezra. He and Evania were as close as brothers. He raised my father as his own and treated me no differently from his other grandkids."

Ellen leaned forward, her pulse quickening. "Excuse me, sir," she interrupted. "My name is Ellen. I'm one of the investigators who found the remains. We want to arrange a proper burial for your grandfather, so he can finally rest in peace. Can that be done today?"

There was a long pause on the other end, and then Dante's grandfather's voice returned, more troubled this time. "Wait a minute, wait a minute. *Malocchio.* That curse I heard the other day . . . was that the voice of my grandfather from beyond the grave?"

Ellen swallowed, glancing at her friends. "We believe so," she said, her voice steady. "We think reuniting and burying his remains will lift the curse. We need to put him to rest."

Dante's grandfather murmured something in Italian, his voice thick with emotion. Then, in English, he said, "I will call my priest and arrange it as soon as possible. He may not be able to do it today, but I'll let Dante know when we can. May I have the remains? I want to have him cremated, so I can spread his ashes over Ezra's grave."

"Of course," Ellen said. "I'll leave them with Dante."

"I wish the rest of my family who already passed could know that Evania was finally found," Dante's grandfather said solemnly.

"I'm sure they do," Sue said into the phone.

"You know what happened to him?" the old man asked.

Ellen stole a glance at Ken, not wanting to trigger the ghost possessing him. "Yes, but it's a conversation best had in person, Mr. Zadra."

"Of course. Goodbye, then."

"Thank you, Nonno," Dante said softly, ending the call. His eyes were glazed with shock, and he leaned back in his chair, staring at the ceiling as if the weight of generations had suddenly dropped on him.

"You know what happened to Evania?" he asked Ellen and her friends.

Before Ellen could say anything, Ken stood, his face twisted with rage. "So," he spat, turning toward Dante, "you're the descendent of that scoundrel?"

Ellen's heart skipped a beat as she saw Ken's fists clench. Before anyone could react, Ken lunged at Dante, his eyes wild with fury. "It's your blood that's cursed me!"

"Ken, no!" Ellen cried, leaping to her feet.

Sue and Tanya were on their feet, too, rushing to hold Ken back, while Moseby barked loudly, caught up in the chaos. Ellen grabbed Ken's arm, trying to pull him away from Dante, who had pushed himself against the wall, wide-eyed and dumbfounded.

"Get ahold of yourself!" Sue shouted, her voice cutting through the commotion. "We'll put you right back in jail if we have to!"

It took everything they had to restrain Ken, but finally, when Ellen threatened to stop trying to help him with the curse, the man stopped struggling, his breath coming in heavy, ragged gasps. Ellen watched him warily, her heart still racing.

"We're all on the same side," she said, her voice firm but soothing. "We need to focus on breaking the curse, not each other."

Ken glared at Dante for a moment longer, then finally looked away, his shoulders sagging in defeat. "I've been waiting too long for this," he muttered.

"Just be patient a little while longer," Ellen pleaded.

As they filed out of the office and back toward the rental car, Ellen hoped and prayed that Glavo's burial could be arranged today—the sooner the better for everyone.

Later that day, snow-capped mountains surrounding Lone Tree Cemetery loomed in quiet majesty, their peaks glistening beneath a pale blue sky, the sun just beginning its evening descent. A crisp chill laced the air, swirling gently through the congregation gathered around the grave of Ezra Zadra. Ellen stood among them, Moseby nestled quietly in his cloth carrier, his warm body a comforting presence in the cold.

Ellen's breath was steady, but her heart felt heavy with a mixture of emotions. Joy and anxiety filled her chest as she glanced at the group around her—Sue, Tanya, Ken, Robin, Dante, and Dante's family, including his elderly Nonno, Antonio. They had all gathered to finally lay Evania Glavo to rest, to bring peace to a soul that had been lost for so very long—though Ellen and her friends didn't know if they'd been successful in reuniting his remains. They had no proof that the hand bones belonged to Glavo. It was possible that the curse would remain unbroken and Robin's family still in need of liberation from the nightmares that plagued them.

Father Matteo, a solemn-faced priest dressed in flowing robes, stood at the head of the small gathering, his voice soft yet steady as he spoke. "We gather here today to return Evania Glavo to his family. Though he was lost without a trace for many years, he has been found, and now, in God's grace, he can finally rest beside his beloved cousin, Ezra Zadra."

Antonio stepped forward, holding a small urn containing Glavo's ashes. His hands trembled slightly as he knelt beside the grave with the help of his grandsons, Dante and Marco. The sight tugged at Ellen's heart—this man, now well into his eighties, was finally able to bring closure to a chapter of his family's story that had haunted them for generations. With a reverent whisper, Antonio gently poured Glavo's ashes into the soil, covering the ground where his cousin had been laid to rest long ago.

A lump formed in Ellen's throat as she watched the ashes settle into the earth, mingling with the dirt that had sheltered Ezra's remains for decades. Tears pricked at the corners of her eyes, and she swallowed hard. She felt a profound sense of accomplishment that she and her friends had been able to bring this moment to fruition. This was what they had worked for, what they had struggled through darkness to achieve—a moment of peace for a family and, hopefully, for a lost soul.

As Father Matteo continued to pray, Ellen couldn't help but steal a glance at Ken. He stood stiffly at the edge of the group, his face pale and strained. Ellen could still feel Buck Wells's presence lingering, as if the ghost was unwilling to leave. Tanya's gaze flickered toward Ken as well, worry etched in her expression. Even Sue was watching him with deep concern.

Ellen took a deep breath, sensing the time was right to intervene. She stepped forward, catching the attention of Father Matteo and Antonio.

"Excuse me," she said softly. "Would it be alright if I said a few words?"

Father Matteo nodded, stepping back to give her the floor. Antonio gave her a small, encouraging smile.

Ellen folded her hands, closing her eyes for a moment as she collected her thoughts. When she spoke, her voice was clear, filled with gentle authority.

"May the soul of Evania Glavo find peace and joy in this final reunion with his family. And may the lifting of this burden, the reunion of his remains, also lift the curse of the evil eye that has plagued the ghost of Buck Wells, so that he, too, may find peace."

The words hung in the air for a moment, carried on the cold wind as if the mountains themselves were listening.

When Ellen opened her eyes, her heart skipped a beat. Ken was stumbling, his face twisted in pain. A strangled gasp escaped his lips as he suddenly fell toward the ground. His wife, Robin, screamed and lunged toward him, but Dante and his relatives were already there, catching Ken before he hit the earth too hard. His body convulsed, and Ellen's stomach dropped as she saw his eyes roll back in his head, only the whites visible. He was seizing.

"Father, help him!" Robin cried, her voice thick with panic as she clung to Ken's hand.

Father Matteo stepped forward without hesitation, kneeling beside Ken and placing his hands over the man's forehead. "Lord, in your mercy, release this man from all torment and grant him peace," he prayed, his voice strong and unwavering.

Ellen's hands trembled as she fumbled for her phone, quickly dialing 9-1-1. The line rang twice before someone picked up.

"9-1-1, what's your emergency?"

"We need an ambulance at Lone Tree Cemetery," Ellen said, her voice cracking under the weight of her fear. "There's a man having a seizure."

As she spoke, Ken's body suddenly stilled. His violent convulsions ceased, and the tension in the air broke. Ellen paused, staring in disbelief as Ken's eyes fluttered open. He blinked up at the sky, disoriented, then slowly sat up with Dante's help.

Ken looked around, his eyes wide with confusion. "Where am I?" he asked, his voice hoarse, but his own. "What's happening?"

Robin knelt beside him, her face streaked with tears. "Ken," she whispered, her voice shaky. "Oh, Ken, you're back. You've come back to me."

Ellen let out a breath of relief. "Cancel that," Ellen said into the phone. "He's okay." She ended the call and stared at Ken. If Buck Wells had left Ken's body, the curse must have been lifted, right? She supposed she wouldn't know for certain until she slept one more night in Robin's house without nightmares.

Father Matteo stood, placing a hand on Ken's shoulder. "You've been through a trial, my son," he said gently. "But I believe the Lord has brought you back to us."

Ken stared at the ground for a long moment, then slowly nodded, though his expression remained dazed.

Ellen exchanged glances with Sue and Tanya, who looked equally relieved, though a thread of concern lingered in their eyes. They had done everything they could. Now, all they could do was hope that this was the end of the torment—for Ken, for Buck Wells, for Evania Glavo, and for Vincent St. John. Peace, at last, seemed within reach. Only tonight would tell.

<u>CHAPTER SEVENTEEN</u>

Vincent St. John

Wednesday night after Glavo's funeral, Ellen pushed open the front door of the mountain home, the familiar scent of pine and stone washing over her. Her body ached from a long day, and her mind was weighed down by lingering doubts. Moseby darted in ahead of her, nails clicking on the polished wooden floors. He seemed blissfully unaffected by the day's emotional and physical toll, tail wagging as he trotted toward the kitchen.

Sue and Tanya followed behind, their faces reflecting the same tired relief Ellen felt. The three of them had managed to give Dante and his family some peace by uncovering the truth about Evania Glavo, Dante's great-great-grandfather. It had been difficult to reveal to them that their ancestor had arranged the assassination of Arthur Collins, but, interestingly, Dante and his relatives seemed to believe that Evania had been justified in seeking revenge for the family. They were more outraged by the defilement Glavo's remains had endured at the hands of McParland as ordered by Buck Wells.

Despite their success in identifying the remains they'd discovered in the cellar, there was a nagging uncertainty. If the hand bones they had uncovered on Boomerang Hill belonged to someone other than Glavo, they were no closer to lifting the curse.

"Let's just hope tonight clears things up," Tanya muttered, her eyes darting to the shadows beyond the windows.

"Yeah," Sue added. "Though, one way or another, we'll get answers tonight, won't we?"

Ellen nodded absently, bending down to fill Moseby's food bowl. "Hopefully Vincent St. John can help us out with that tonight."

The tension in the air was palpable as they set about their preparations for the night. The dining room had become their makeshift investigation space. Ellen placed three thick candles in the center of the table while Tanya rebuilt a fire in the hearth.

Sue moved around the room, setting up the rest of their equipment—an EVP recorder, EMF meters, and full-spectrum cameras. Ellen caught Sue's eye and gave her a tired smile. They were close, she could feel it. But close wasn't good enough—not when lives, both living and dead, were involved.

Ellen lit the three candles, their flames dancing delicately in the still air. She felt a knot of tension ease slightly as the warm glow filled the space. She turned to the enormous Christmas tree near the floor-to-ceiling windows. The tree was a comforting sight amid her uncertainty.

"Let's get started," she said with a sigh.

The three of them took their seats around the table—Ellen in the middle at the head of the table. Moseby returned to his place on the sofa across from the hearth, now glowing with dancing flames.

Ellen took a deep breath, centering herself before speaking into the dimly lit room, "We call upon the spirit of Vincent St. John. We ask for your presence and your guidance. If you are here with us, Vincent, please give us a sign."

For a moment, there was nothing but the steady hum of silence. Then, the EMF meter on the table flickered, the lights pulsing faintly.

Ellen leaned forward slightly, heart beating faster. "Vincent, if you can hear us, we need your help. Please, knock once for yes and twice for no."

The room held its breath. A single, sharp knock echoed from somewhere beneath the floorboards.

Ellen exchanged a glance with Sue and Tanya.

"That's a yes," Sue whispered.

Ellen steadied herself and continued, "Is the spirit of Buck Wells still tethered to this house? Is he still in the cellar?"

Two knocks.

"No," Tanya murmured, eyes wide with realization. "He's gone."

"Thank goodness," Sue murmured. "I'd had about enough of him."

"Vincent, can you tell us if Buck's spirit has moved on?" Ellen asked, her voice hushed.

One knock.

Ellen felt a rush of hope flood her chest. "And Evania Glavo? Has his spirit moved on as well?"

One knock.

A wave of relief washed over the room, palpable and thick. Ellen let out a breath of relief. They had done it. They had lifted the curse and had helped Glavo and Buck find peace.

Ellen smiled, glancing at her friends. "Vincent, thank you. Truly. You've given us the closure we needed. Now, it's time for us to help you."

They began with the "Lord's Prayer," the familiar words flowing between them like a practiced melody.

Then, Ellen said, "Vincent St. John, we call upon your loved ones who have passed. We call upon your sister, Helen, and your wife, Clara. Lead Vincent to the light. Show him the way."

For several moments, the room remained silent, the candles' soft glow filling the space. Then, without warning, two of the three candles snuffed out, plunging them into near darkness. Ellen's heart raced, but she kept her composure. The air felt lighter, the oppressive weight that had pressed down on the house since their arrival lifting at last.

"He's gone," Sue whispered, awe in her voice.

Ellen nodded, a smile tugging at her lips. "I think we've done it. Saint is finally at peace."

The three of them sat there for a few moments longer, basking in the stillness of the room. For the first time since they had arrived at the mountain home, the house felt peaceful. No shadows lurking in the corners, no weight of unresolved spirits pressing down on them.

They had succeeded, but Ellen knew they wouldn't be certain until they had spent the night free of the nightmares that had plagued them since their arrival—nightmares that had tormented Robin and her family as well. The house felt different, better, but they wouldn't truly know until morning.

"Let's call it a night," Tanya suggested, rising from the table.

Ellen stood and blew out the remaining candle, the last wisp of smoke curling into the air. "Here's to a peaceful night."

With hope in her heart, she headed upstairs, the weight of the day behind her.

"Come on, Moseby-Mo," Ellen called to her dog. "Let's go to bed."

Ellen awoke to the soft, rhythmic sound of Moseby licking her face. The gentle tickle of his warm tongue stirred her from sleep, and she groggily wiped her eyes. "Moseby, what are you doing?" she muttered, voice thick with the remnants of dreams. But Moseby persisted, his insistent nudging telling her something was wrong—or, at the very least, important.

With a sigh, she swung her legs out of bed and shuffled to her feet, Moseby already trotting ahead, his tail wagging as if beckoning her to follow. The house was quiet, still cloaked in the early morning darkness. Ellen rubbed the back of her neck, yawning as she followed the little dog down the hall, her bare feet brushing softly against the hardwood floor. She wasn't sure why Moseby was leading her to the office, but something tugged at her gut, that familiar sensation she had learned to trust.

The office door was slightly ajar, and when she pushed it open, the whiteboard on the far wall caught her attention. Their timeline of events and notes from their days of work still crowded the board, scribbled in messy black marker. But there—between hastily written ideas and crossed-out theories—was something new.

THANK YOU, V

Ellen blinked, her heart skipping a beat as she stared at the words, written clearly in bold, black strokes, in writing unlike Tanya's or

Sue's. A chill ran down her spine. She stepped closer, her breath catching as she realized what this meant.

Vincent St. John.

The words seemed to glow in the dim morning light filtering through the office window. Gratitude, simple and undeniable, written by the hand of a ghost. St. John had crossed over, just as they had hoped, and he'd left a message behind.

"Moseby," she whispered, her voice trembling with awe. The little dog sat at her feet, tail swishing across the floor as if he, too, understood the significance of the moment. Ellen reached out, fingers hovering above the board, but just as she was about to touch the words—

She woke up.

Her heart pounded as she blinked against the morning light streaming through her bedroom windows. It had been a dream, vivid and real enough to pull her from sleep. But Moseby was there, sitting patiently at the foot of her bed, tail wagging as though waiting for her to get up. Ellen sat up quickly, wiping her brow. The dream had felt so real, the thank-you so clear, so personal.

Without thinking, she jumped out of bed, Moseby barking with excitement as he followed her down the hallway. Her mind raced. She knew it had been a dream, but she couldn't shake the feeling that something more was at play. Could it have been a sign?

When she reached the office, Ellen hesitated for a moment before pushing the door open. Her breath caught in her throat. The whiteboard was just as they had left it, filled with their notes and crossed-out ideas—but no thank-you message. No Vincent St. John.

Disappointment settled in her chest like a heavy weight. Of course, it had only been a dream. What had she expected? A ghost's handwritten thank you in black marker? She let out a small sigh, ready to leave the office, but something stopped her. A flicker of light caught her eye.

She stepped closer to the board, squinting at the upper corner. There, within the written words of their timeline, was something faint. Ellen leaned in, her pulse quickening as she realized what she was seeing. It wasn't written in marker, but in the erased space. "THANK YOU, V" was barely visible, like someone had run their finger through the remnants of the dry-erase ink.

Her breath hitched as her eyes widened. It was there. St. John had left a message after all—just not the way she had dreamt. She could almost feel the ghost's lingering presence, his gratitude etched in the faintest of traces.

"Moseby," she whispered, voice filled with awe.

The dog's ears perked up as if sensing the importance of the discovery.

Ellen reached out, fingers tracing the faint outline of the letters. A broad smile broke across her face as the realization sank in. Vincent St. John had thanked them. He had truly crossed over, and he had left this message behind to let them know.

She couldn't wait to tell the others.

"What's going on?" Tanya asked sleepily from the doorway. "What's Moseby happy about?"

"You and Sue need to see this," Ellen said with a voice full of excitement.

"What do I need to see?" Sue asked as she reached the hall behind Tanya.

"Wait a minute." Tanya moved toward the whiteboard. "I had a dream about this."

"Me, too," Sue said, following. "Vincent St. John left a message."

"It's here." Ellen pointed at the board. "See it?"

"Oh, now I do," Tanya said with awe. "That's amazing."

"Incredible," Sue agreed. "Are you sure you didn't do that, Ellen?"

"I promise I didn't," Ellen insisted.

"Now we know it's really over," Tanya said. "It's time to celebrate."

"Should we have our Christmas party tonight?" Sue wondered.

"Absolutely," Ellen said with a clap of her hands, causing Moseby to jump at her feet and wag his tail.

Tanya put her hands on her hips. "What if we drive into Telluride and take the gondola to Mountain Village for lunch, finish our last-minute shopping, and then pick up something to eat here before we open our presents?"

"Sounds like a plan!" Ellen beamed.

"I'll start researching new places to eat," Sue offered.

Tanya and Ellen grinned at one another.

"She really is the smart one," Ellen said.

Tanya nodded. "I was just about to say that."

CHAPTER EIGHTEEN

Christmas Presents

Ellen stepped through the front door of Robin's mountain home, instantly enveloped by the warmth and comfort of the familiar space. It had been a delightful afternoon of lunching and shopping in Telluride and Mountain Village with Sue and Tanya. The festive town, with its twinkling Christmas lights, snow-covered streets, and the gondola ride between the villages, had felt like a winter wonderland. Yet Ellen was happy to return to the serenity of the house, especially now that their supernatural troubles seemed to be behind them.

"Moseby!" Ellen called as she stepped inside. "Did you miss me, boy? Let's go outside."

The tiny black dog trotted toward her from his favorite spot by the fireplace, tail wagging. She opened the door and let him out off-leash, watching as he dashed toward the firs and pines surrounding the house. Stepping outside herself, Ellen took in the breathtaking scenery. The sun was beginning to dip behind the mountains, casting a warm glow across the snow. The air was crisp, tinged with the earthy scent of evergreens.

For the first time in weeks, Ellen felt an overwhelming sense of peace. No more tethered ghosts, no more nightmares, and no more curses. Just the mountains, her friends, and Moseby happily exploring.

The sight of him sniffing around the trees made her smile. She took a deep breath, savoring the tranquility that dusk brought to the landscape. How beautiful it was here, and how blessed she felt to be able to enjoy it without the weight of the past haunting her.

"Moseby!" she called after a while. "Time to come inside, boy!"

The dog came running back, and Ellen scooped him up with a laugh, his warmth comforting in the cool air. Inside, Sue and Tanya had already disappeared into their rooms, likely wrapping the gifts with the paper and ribbons they had bought that afternoon. Ellen retreated to her own room to do the same, still smiling at the quiet contentment of the moment.

Ellen emerged from her room a half-hour later with her arms full of neatly wrapped gifts and Moseby trailing faithfully behind her. She navigated the stairs carefully, the scent of pine and cinnamon filling the air from the Christmas decorations. As she descended to the main floor, she could hear the familiar strains of "White Christmas" playing from the television mounted over the fireplace. Sue, standing by the Christmas tree, was singing along with her arms stretched wide, clearly in her element.

Tanya, kneeling by the tree, chuckled at Sue's theatrics. She added the last of her wrapped presents to the collection beneath the tree and glanced up just as Ellen approached.

"Perfect timing!" Tanya said with a grin, adjusting the position of one of the brightly colored packages. "Look at all these gifts. We've outdone ourselves this year."

Sue, still humming, finally stopped to join in. "Every year, we say that. And every year, it's true!"

Ellen placed her gifts under the tree, the gold ribbon on one of the packages catching the light from the twinkling fairy lights. This was a tradition she and her friends shared every year, inspired by *The Oprah Winfrey Show*. They each pick out two of their favorite things to buy for their friends.

"Who wants to start?" Sue asked, her voice excited.

"I will!" Ellen said, plucking two of her gifts from beneath the tree. She handed one each to Sue and Tanya. "You might not be able to tell what these are, so I'll explain once you open them."

Tanya tore into hers, holding up a set of matching fabric pieces, her brow furrowed in curiosity. Sue did the same, revealing a similar set in a different pattern.

"Are these . . . potholders?" Tanya asked.

Ellen smiled. "Sort of. They're bowl cozies for the microwave. You put them under a bowl before heating it, and they make it easy to take the hot bowl out without burning yourself. I even keep them on while I eat, so I can hold the bowl closer to my mouth."

Sue clapped her hands together. "Brilliant! And they match my kitchen colors perfectly. I love them!"

"I thought you'd like them," Ellen said, pleased. "I use mine all the time. And they're machine washable."

Tanya nodded appreciatively. "These are amazing, Ellen. Thank you!"

Next, Ellen handed over her second set of gifts.

After unwrapping hers, Sue gasped, holding hers up. "Is this a Jenni Bag? I've been wanting one of these! I've seen the ads all over my Facebook feed."

Ellen beamed. "Yes, it is. I can fit so much into mine, and it keeps everything so organized. I figured you'd love it."

Tanya ran her fingers over the bag's fabric. "I've nearly bought one a dozen times. I can't wait to try it out!"

"My turn now," Tanya insisted, her eyes sparkling with excitement as she reached under the tree to grab two small packages. She handed one to Ellen and the other to Sue. Ellen carefully peeled away the wrapping paper, revealing a slim, sleek tube of mascara. Sue, already halfway through unwrapping hers, grinned as she held up an identical tube.

"This is the only mascara I've ever used that doesn't smudge but washes off easily," Tanya explained, her tone confident. "I swear by it."

Sue leaned closer to examine the tube, her expression thoughtful. "I absolutely need this in my life. My eyes are always smudgy by noon—it's like a curse. But, no more! Thanks, Tanya!" she added with a grin.

Ellen nodded in agreement, twisting the cap of the mascara open and looking at the brush. "I've been on the hunt for something like this. I hate when mascara turns me into a raccoon halfway through the day. Thank you, Tanya!"

"You're welcome!" Tanya smiled, pleased by their reactions. "Trust me, once you use it, you'll wonder how you ever lived without it."

They shared a laugh, the warm glow of the Christmas tree lights reflecting off their gift boxes. Tanya wasn't finished, though. She reached back under the tree, producing two larger gifts wrapped in elegant silver paper.

Ellen unwrapped her package slowly, savoring the moment. Inside was a beautiful, tan cardigan made of the softest cashmere she had ever felt. She gasped slightly, running her fingers over the luxurious fabric. Sue had received a black one and was already holding it up to admire the cut.

"This is the softest and most flattering sweater I have ever owned," Tanya explained. "I hope I got the right sizes."

Sue slipped hers on immediately, the black cashmere hugging her figure in all the right places. "It fits perfectly!" she exclaimed. "And it really is soft."

Ellen followed suit, slipping the tan cardigan over her shoulders. The warmth of the cashmere enveloped her, and she couldn't help but admire how the soft material draped down her arms. "It's fabulous, Tanya," she said, smiling as she gave the sleeves a little tug. "Thank you so much. It's perfect."

Tanya beamed, her own eyes twinkling with pride at having chosen the perfect gifts. "I'm so glad you both like them."

Sue twirled slightly, showing off the sweater. "I may never take this off. It's perfect for cold nights like these."

Ellen nodded, already imagining herself cozying up with a book by the fire while wearing her new cardigan. The feel of it was almost too good to be true.

"Last but not least!" Sue chirped cheerfully, breaking the cozy silence. She handed her first gifts to Ellen and Tanya, her expression one of anticipation.

Ellen unwrapped her small box, revealing a tiny jar of eye cream.

Sue leaned forward eagerly. "This is the only product I have found that gets rid of eye bags," she said. "Have y'all noticed that my bags aren't as noticeable as they used to be?"

Ellen studied Sue's face. "I have noticed," she said with a nod. "Your skin looks great."

"Oh, I need this so much," Tanya said, holding the small jar delicately. "My bags have been bringing me down lately. Thank you, Sue!"

Sue grinned, pleased with the positive feedback. "It's a miracle in a jar, I swear."

Before Ellen could say more, Sue handed over her second gift, a larger box that felt oddly light. Ellen unwrapped it and pulled out a pair of black Crocs. But these weren't the typical Crocs. They were wedge heels with ankle straps, sleek and surprisingly stylish.

Sue beamed. "I know it's too cold to wear these here in Colorado, but back home in San Antonio, you might wear them soon enough. They're the most comfortable shoes I've ever worn. And I think they're pretty, too. Don't you think?"

Ellen laughed, already kicking off her boots and socks. "Let's find out."

She slipped her feet into the wedge Crocs and stood up. They fit perfectly, hugging her feet in just the right way. Ellen let out a contented sigh. "You're right, Sue. These are so comfortable! And they look cute. I'm impressed."

"We made out good this year, didn't we?" Tanya said with a smile. "Though, I guess we do every year," she added, with a hint of a chuckle.

Ellen glanced around at the wrapping paper strewn across the floor, the brightly colored gifts under the tree, and her friends laughing and smiling. "Yeah, we really did."

They reminisced about Christmases past—Sue's disastrous attempt at making a gingerbread house last year, Tanya's obsession with finding the perfect gift-wrap, Ellen's infamous Christmas dinner that ended in takeout after a burnt turkey. Laughter filled the room as they shared the memories, the warmth of their friendship glowing brighter than the tree itself.

Just as Sue had finished telling another humorous story about her mother—about the time she sprayed lemon Pledge on the artificial Christmas tree because she had run out of Pinesol, and their guests were stumped by the lemony smell while Sue was fearful of a fire—Tanya's phone rang.

"Dave? Everything alright?" Tanya, surprised to hear from him, said into the phone. "Yes, in a few days. We leave for Santa Fe tomorrow . . . What? . . . Liar. That's not funny . . . You're serious? . . . This better not be a joke . . . Really? Truly? . . . I'll believe it when I see it . . . Okay, see you soon . . . I love you, too."

By the time Tanya had ended the call, her eyes were filled with tears.

"Everything okay?" Sue asked.

"Tanya?" Ellen put a comforting hand on her friend's shoulder. "What's going on?"

"Dave said we had a cancellation at our Biloxi rental house for the week of Christmas," Tanya began, "and he's arranged for us and the kids to spend the week there together." Tanya's tears spilled down her cheeks. "I just can't believe it."

"Oh, Tanya!" Sue lifted her brows. "That's great news."

"You guys will have such a good time there," Ellen agreed. "What a nice place to spend Christmas together."

"I was afraid we wouldn't have a Christmas," Tanya admitted. "Dave had talked about needing to be in D.C. I'm still not sure I believe him."

"He's making an effort," Sue pointed out, "and that counts for something, doesn't it?"

"It shows he cares," Ellen added. "You're important to him."

Tanya nodded. "Yes, it does show he cares. I'm still in shock, to be honest."

In her hyperbolic way, Sue spread her arms wide. "It's a Christmas miracle!"

Later, after clearing away the discarded wrapping paper and tucking their gifts under the tree, the trio made their way to the kitchen. "Jingle Bells" played over the television as they began warming up the dinner they'd picked up in Telluride. The scent of roasted chicken and garlic mashed potatoes filled the kitchen, and before long, they were all singing along to the music, their voices harmonizing, albeit off-key, as they prepared their plates.

Ellen paused for a moment, watching her friends with affection. Tanya, still humming, sliced into the chicken, while Sue danced in place, swinging her arms as if the holiday cheer had taken over her body. Ellen felt a wave of emotion swell up inside her, the happiness so pure it brought tears to her eyes.

As they sat down together at the table, Ellen quietly wiped away the happy tears and thought, *How blessed I am to have such good friends to share these times with.*

CHAPTER NINETEEN

Goodbye Telluride

Ellen sat at the kitchen bar, cradling her mug of steaming coffee in both hands. Outside the windows, snow blanketed the rugged landscape. Inside, warmth radiated from the stone fireplace, and the scent of toasted bagels filled the air. Moseby chomped away at his breakfast on the floor nearby, oblivious to the conversation that buzzed above him.

Sue stood beside Ellen, holding a bagel and slathering it with cream cheese. "You know," Sue began, eyeing the three neatly wrapped gifts beneath the small, tastefully decorated Christmas tree, "I've been staring at those presents all morning. What's the deal, Ellen? You hiding something good?"

Ellen glanced at the tree, then smiled. "Those are the dreamcatchers I bought for my grandkids when we shopped in Santa Fe."

Tanya raised an eyebrow. "Oh? And here I thought you had one more surprise for each of us."

Sue chuckled, sipping her coffee. "Someone ought to invent hot-flash catchers. I'd have one hanging above my bed, one in the car, and probably one around my neck."

Ellen shook her head, grinning. "I think I'm going to leave them here for Robin and her kids, to give them an extra reassurance that the nightmares are over. Besides, I'll have plenty of time to get new ones when we swing by Santa Fe on our way home to San Antonio."

"That's sweet," Tanya said, tearing off a piece of her bagel. "Speaking of Robin, what time are they supposed to get here?"

"She said noon," Sue replied.

Ellen nodded. "So, we've got a few hours to shower, dress, pack, and maybe do a quick tidy-up. You know, make the place look like we're not a bunch of menopausal wrecks who left their bras hanging over the shower rods."

Tanya snorted. "Speak for yourself. I gave up on bras years ago. There's a kind of freedom in letting nature do its thing."

Sue cupped her bosom. "That's because you don't have these puppies here. If I could barely fill a B-cup, I'd go braless, too."

Ellen smiled, feeling a sense of lightness that had nothing to do with the jokes. She'd had the best night's sleep of the trip—no nightmares, no uneasy feeling of being watched. Just deep, peaceful sleep.

"How did y'all sleep last night?" she asked her friends.

"Great," Tanya said. "And I loved taking my time this morning to admire the view. I almost wish we had another few days here."

"It was nice, wasn't it?" Ellen agreed. "Knowing that the curse is finally lifted. Vincent St. John, Buck Wells, and Evania Glavo—at peace, all of them."

Sue nodded, her expression softening. "Yeah, I feel it too. The whole house feels . . . lighter. Like it's breathing again."

"Just in time for Christmas," Tanya added with a smile.

Moseby wandered over to Ellen's feet, nosing at her leg. She bent down, scratching behind his ears. "Even Moseby slept through the night, didn't you, boy?"

"Well," Tanya said, glancing at the clock on the wall, "as much as I'd love to sit here all day and soak in the peaceful vibes, I suppose we should get moving if we want to be ready when Robin and her family arrive."

"I suppose we should," Ellen agreed. "I'll put these mugs and silverware in the dishwasher. Maybe we could also wipe down our bathrooms?"

Sue groaned dramatically. "Do we *have* to? I don't even do that in my own home—I hire other people. And I think they'd be fine if we didn't, since we just made it possible for them to keep this beautiful home."

Ellen rolled her eyes. "Would it kill you to tidy up just a little?"

"I think it might," Sue teased, "but I'll do it anyway. Be thinking of something good to put on my tombstone."

"Maybe we should also put our bedding in the laundry room," Tanya said, ignoring Sue's joke.

Sue threw her hands up in mock surrender. "Fine, fine. But don't expect me to fold any fitted sheets. I'll take the ghosts over those demons any day."

The three of them laughed, the sound filling the cozy kitchen as the last remnants of tension melted away. Ellen took a deep breath, glancing once more at the snow outside. For the first time in what felt like forever, everything was calm. Peaceful. Just like the souls they had helped find rest.

Ellen zipped up her bag and took a deep breath, gazing out at the snow-dusted landscape one last time before closing the back hatch of the rental car. The mountains loomed majestically in the distance, and the chilly air was crisp, carrying the smell of pine. Sue and Tanya were busy checking the car's interior for any last-minute items they might have missed, and Moseby, having already taken his seat, peered out from the back, watching intently.

"Everything in?" Sue asked, pushing her dark bangs from her eyes.

"Yep, all good," Ellen confirmed.

Just as they were about to return inside to make one more walk-through, the low hum of another car came up the drive. Ellen turned to see a familiar SUV making its way toward them. Robin and her family had arrived back home.

"Right on time," Tanya said, waving at the approaching car.

The SUV parked next to their rental, and out spilled Robin, Ken, and their two kids, Dex and Sophie, bundled in their winter coats. A burst of excitement followed as the children rushed over, eager to show off their newest family member—a wriggling Golden Retriever puppy with an oversized, red ribbon tied around its neck.

"Oh, how adorable!" Ellen exclaimed, crouching to pet the puppy, who was wagging his tail so enthusiastically that his whole body wiggled.

"This is Max," Dex announced proudly. "We just got him this morning!"

Moseby, curious as ever, hopped out of the car and trotted over, sniffing the puppy. Within seconds, the two dogs were engaged in a playful bout of sniffing, circling, and gentle pawing. Ellen's heart warmed as she watched them tumble around on the melting snow, their antics so cute that everyone was laughing.

"Looks like Moseby's made a new friend," Sue said, grinning at the pair. "And Ken, it's nice to see you looking like yourself again." She winked, prompting Ken to chuckle.

"Well, I definitely feel more like myself," Ken replied, his expression grateful but still a bit tired.

Inside the house, the fire crackled warmly. The Christmas tree sparkled with lights and ornaments and beneath it lay the three wrapped gifts Ellen had left.

"I left some presents under the tree for you all," Ellen said, nodding toward the colorful packages. "Something to remember us by."

Robin and Ken exchanged a look, their faces softening with gratitude. "Ellen, Sue, and Tanya," Robin began, her voice thick with emotion, "we can never thank you enough for everything you have done for us. I don't even know how we could ever repay you."

Tanya, folding her arms with a warm smile, chimed in, "It was truly a blessing to stay in your beautiful home and to see parts of Colorado I'd never experienced before—it's been an unforgettable trip."

Robin carefully reached into her bag and pulled out three neatly folded t-shirts. "I wanted to give you something to remember us by," she said, handing one to each of them. The shirts read *I Love Telluride* in bold letters. "Hopefully, you'll wear them and think of us."

"We'll definitely wear these," Ellen said, pulling hers close to her chest. "And speaking of memories, we left up the timeline we created in the office. You might find it interesting."

Robin and Ken looked at her quizzically, and Ellen explained, "We put together what we believe happened—how Evania Glavo paid

Canun Siti to assassinate Arthur Collins, and how Buck Wells, after hearing Glavo's confession, killed him and passed off his remains as those of William J. Barney to indict Vincent St. John."

"Wow," Ken said, rubbing his chin. "That's . . . a lot."

"We've already sent photos of the timeline and a report to both the director of the Telluride Museum and the chief of police," Ellen continued. "Not sure what they'll do with it, but Sue has posted the same report on her blog, and it's gotten attention from local historians."

Sue grinned mischievously. "Always stirring the pot."

With their goodbyes exchanged and hugs all around, Ellen scooped up Moseby, whose winter sweater was still damp from the snow, and she and her friends climbed into their rental car. Sue climbed behind the wheel, with Tanya beside her, and Ellen settled in the back, Moseby nestled comfortably in her lap.

As they drove away from the house, Ellen gazed out the window at the passing snowy landscape, her heart tugging with bittersweet fondness. "I'm going to miss this place," she admitted softly.

"Me too," Tanya said, her eyes forward. "Especially the hike in the Box Canyon Springs of Ouray. That was magical."

Sue chuckled from the driver's seat. "For me, it was the shopping in Mountain Village. You can never have too many scarves, and I love the ornament I picked out to remember this trip by."

"I love mine, too," Ellen said. "But the gondola ride was my favorite. There's something about being up there, looking over everything—it just gives you perspective, you know?"

"Speaking of perspectives," Sue said, tapping the dashboard, "Tanya, can you search for good places to eat in Durango? I'm thinking it might be a nice spot to stop for lunch."

Tanya pulled out her phone and began scrolling through options, but before she could speak, the dashboard lit up with an incoming call.

"Looks like we're getting a call," Sue said, glancing at the screen. She pressed the answer button and said, "Hello?"

"Is this Sue Graham with Ghost Healers, Inc.?" the voice asked.

"Yes, this is Sue. I'm here with my team, Tanya and Ellen. Who's calling?"

"This is John Coleman with the Henry Ford Museum in Dearborn, Michigan. Maybe you've heard of us?"

Sue perked up. "Yes, I've been wanting to visit."

"I'm glad to hear that, Mrs. Graham, because I'd like to offer you and your team complimentary tickets and a free stay to come help us like you've done at the other places you mention on your blog."

Sue exchanged a curious look with Tanya. "What seems to be the problem?"

"I'd rather not discuss too much over the phone," John replied, his voice lowering. "Let's just say our windmill won't stop whispering."

Ellen leaned forward, intrigued. "Have you had an engineer take a look at it? There could be a logical explanation."

"I've hired more people than you can count on both hands," John said, his frustration clear. "We're desperate here. Our admission numbers are down, and we want to nip this in the bud before ghost stories start spreading. We're a family-friendly park, but lately, the bulk of our visitors are ghost hunters—no offense."

The three women exchanged excited looks. Sue bit her lip and said, "Let us think about it and get back to you tomorrow. When were you needing us to come out there?"

"We're closed for the first time in decades but hope to reopen in March. We'd love to have you come out here before then."

"I'll call you tomorrow, after we've had a chance to discuss it, Mr. Coleman."

"Sounds good, Mrs. Graham. Thank you."

After ending the call, she turned to her friends. "So, what do you think? Are we ready to do this again?"

Ellen grinned. "You bet your bottom dollar we are."

"Agreed," Tanya added with a gleam in her eye. "Dearborn, Michigan, here we come!"

***

THE END

Thank you for reading my story. I hope you enjoyed it! If you did, please consider leaving a review. Reviews help other readers to discover my books, which helps me.

Please visit my website at evapohler.com to get the next book, *The Whispering Windmill.*

EVA POHLER

Eva Pohler is a *USA Today* bestselling author of over forty novels in multiple genres, including ghost mysteries, thrillers, and young adult paranormal romance based on Greek mythology. Her books have been described as "addictive" and "sure to thrill"—*Kirkus Reviews*.

To learn more about Eva and her books, to receive a free ebook, and to sign up to hear about new releases and sales, please visit her website at https://www.evapohler.com.

Acknowledgments

I would like to thank these premium members for their continual support:

Amie Boutte

Lori Brooks

Theresa Christ

Rebekka and Sherry Colegrove

Amanda Ecker

Kerry Erickson

Jessica Garza

Venette Grisham

Samie Hall-Rood

Shellie Hedge

Misty Killion

Anita Klaboe

Leslie Lawrence

Samantha Lundergan

Carrie McCauley

Patrick Mitchell

Glorianna Murry

Liana Petrone

Rachel Renzo

Patricia Hand Salinas

Candy Smith

Debi Vap

Kimberly Walls

Kristi Yates